For
Kelsey Davis
F. Burleigh Willard Sr.

JASON
– OF –
TARSUS

by

F. Burleigh Willard Sr.

authorHOUSE®

AuthorHouse™
1663 Liberty Drive
Bloomington, IN 47403
www.authorhouse.com
Phone: 1-800-839-8640

First published by AuthorHouse 1/8/2010

ISBN: 978-1-4490-4529-6 (e)
ISBN: 978-1-4490-4527-2 (sc)
ISBN: 978-1-4490-4528-9 (hc)

Library of Congress Control Number: 2009913906

Printed in the United States of America
Bloomington, Indiana

This book is printed on acid-free paper.

For more information, please contact:

F. Burleigh Willard
P.O. Box 182
Lincoln, IL 62656
wlmlbooks@msn.com

Dedication

To the pastors and members of Neighbors to Nations Community Church who have encouraged me to keep serving the Lord with my writing. They have supported me with their prayers and given me positive feedback on each book I have written during my four years among them in Lincoln, Illinois.

CONTENTS

ACKNOWLEDGEMENTS

I owe the idea for this book to two other authors. My encounter, during seminary days, with William Ramsay's excellent books, *The Cities of St. Paul* and *St. Paul the Traveller and the Roman Citizen*, whetted my appetite to know more about the life and times of the Apostle Paul. At about the same time, Henry Van Dyke's *The Story of the Other Wise Man* inspired me with the possibility of filling in the blanks in biblical stories with a narrative of what might have happened. I began researching the culture and geography surrounding various scriptural personalities. The first fruit of that study and imagination was *Friend of Angels*, a book which follows Joseph to Egypt and back in his important role as earthly father of Jesus. And now, many years after filling out note cards on the subject, I have the satisfaction of writing a story of the hidden years of St. Paul's life, through the eyes of his nephew.

Many thanks to my daughter, Celia, without whose assistance this project would not have been accomplished. She helped me to rework the mostly-informative rough draft of this story, transforming it into a work of fiction with reader appeal. In addition, her computer and business skills created a finished manuscript and handled the details of getting it published.

I appreciate the staff at AuthorHouse for their gracious and expert guidance through the publishing process.

I am grateful to the Lord for inspiration all along the way and for the health to complete this task. May the resulting book be a blessing to those who read it.

Introduction

Because of his many epistles and Luke's narrative of his journeys, we know more about Paul's ministry and the places he visited than of any of the other apostles. We know very little, however, about his life before his conversion on the road to Damascus, the importance of the cities where he ministered, or his life between his acquittal and his second trial, which resulted in his execution.

It is the purpose of this treatise to shed light on these very important parts of the life of the Apostle Paul which will help us understand some of the puzzling statements and actions of this dynamic person. This will be presented in the form of a novel of the life of Saul of Tarsus as seen through the eyes of Jason of Tarsus—a nephew of the great apostle who with the rest of his family were pained and puzzled at the actions of their famous (or infamous) relative.

Surprisingly, since Saul was undoubtedly repudiated by his devoutly Jewish family after his conversion on the road to Damascus, the apostle greets a total of seven members of his family as his companions in Romans 16:7, 16:11; 16:21 and Acts 19:22. We are also told in Acts 23:16 that it was the son of Saul's sister (his nephew) who heard of the plot to kill Saul and who took the news, first to Saul and then to the commander of the Roman soldiers. Of the relatives named by Saul in Romans 16, I have chosen Jason and cast him as the main representative of the family business whose journeys take him in the footsteps of Saul (without knowing it at first) until he is finally convinced of his sincerity and converted to his Christian faith. So we will be seeing Saul and his ministry through the eyes of this fictionalized nephew Jason.

This outline of the "hidden years" of Paul's life is of course based on conjecture, but, in the concept of the author, is supported by rational conclusions made after a careful study of Jews in Tarsus, Rome and Spain in Paul's time and of Paul's travels on his missionary journeys as carefully documented by William M. Ramsey in his excellent volumes *St. Paul, the Traveler and Roman Citizen* and *The Cities of St. Paul.*[1]

Chapter I
Early life in Tarsus

Jason paced the deck of the Roman grain ship as it sailed along the northern shore of the Mediterranean Sea. They were approaching the eastern end of the sea and he could now see the towering Taurus Mountains that he knew overlooked his home in Tarsus. Soon he could see the mouth of the Cydnus River as it emptied into the sea. Beyond it were the lake and plowed fields that led to the city itself.

But the most remarkable sight of all was the deep gorge of the river as it plunged hundreds of feet in a series of waterfalls down the precipitous ravine which at places was so narrow that the water washed the rocks on both sides of the narrow passage. Despite the sheer drop from the tableland above the city, a narrow and dangerous trail, known as the Cilician Gates, had been carved out from the steep walls. These walls were marked with caves that gave shelter to the caravans and travelers. They also furnished hiding places for robbers who infested the route to plunder the rich caravans from the East.

So Roman soldiers were employed in guarding these rich cargoes of spices and silk.

As Jason became more and more excited about soon reaching home, he was surprised to hear the voice of his new friend Antonio with whom he had whiled away many hours on this homeward voyage.

"Ho, Jason, what are you getting so excited about?"

"Excited? Of course I'm excited. I'm almost home!"

"I don't see any town. Where is Tarsus?"

"It will come into sight any time now, but just look at the view. Do you see those high snow capped mountains over there to the left?"

"Yes, what mountains are those?"

"That is Mount Taurus. You see, it is still snow-capped this late in the summer. The melting snow from that mountain is what rushes across the tableland you see here on our left. We will soon see the point where the water from the snow melt falls over the edge of the highlands, carving out a deep, vertical canyon. From there, the water falls into a basin just back of the city of Tarsus, and then runs on out to sea, forming a rich delta. The wonderful vegetables and fruits that grow there make life pleasant and prosperous in Tarsus."

"That sounds great, but I don't see how that makes it such an important city."

"Well, to understand that you need to know that the Greeks, and later the Romans, decided to choose strategically located cities and make them showcases of Greek and Roman culture. In order to do this they assembled tradesmen, merchants, and artisans to make the city prosperous and diverse—just as they believed that Roman cities are. With this in mind, they gave Roman citizenship to all the inhabitants of these new cities. Tarsus was chosen as one of those new Roman cities. My family, whose trade is tent-making, was chosen as some of the new residents of Tarsus. With our trade we have helped make Tarsus a prosperous city. You know we are Jews, but by royal decree we are also Roman citizens."

"That is very interesting, but why did they choose Tarsus? I hope you won't think I am critical of your city, but it seems to be in a strange, out-of-the-way place."

"You may think so now but wait until you see the marvelous link we have with the high road through Asia Minor. The high road is the main route for the spices and silk of the East on their way to Greece and Rome."

"I am aware of that, but why is the dangerous road down that horrible gulch any better than the highway through Asia Minor?"

"Because it is short and can easily be defended by Roman soldiers. Then the goods can be loaded on ships and sail anywhere to Greece and Italy. It is not only a quicker route, but bypasses the long, brigand-infested highway through Asia Minor, and the dangerous and difficult sea lanes through the Aegean Sea and around Greece."

"But that is not the only reason for the importance of Tarsus," continued Jason. "It has also become the seat of Western culture between Palestine and Europe. Its university is not of a size or reputation to rival Antioch or Alexandria, but it does boast of famous teachers from those universities who regularly visit the city to teach its eager students. I am not only a graduate of our synagogue schools, but also of the Greek university just as my Uncle Saul was. I speak the languages of Greece and Rome as well as Hebrew. This, along with my Roman citizenship, gives me free access to the entire Roman world."

"Tell me more about your business and your part in the enterprise."

"Our business is tent-making. You probably know that the Jewish people are known, not for farming the soil, but for their large herds of sheep and goats. They had to move about constantly, because the herds soon cropped all the grass in one location, so the families and their herds were always moving from one place to another. By living in tents, woven from the fleece of their herds, they were able to take living quarters with them and pitch them in their new location. We provided the tents for our nomadic people.

"But we have found that with the growth of cities and the cultivation of the land for crops of corn, wheat and vegetables, we are loosing our ability to move freely to more fertile land. As a result, our business has been losing clients amazingly fast, and we are forced to find new clients or go bankrupt. It was in searching for new clients that I discovered that the Roman army, especially on the frontiers, used an enormous amount of tents. It was then that I began taking orders for army tents, and am now returning home to bring new life to our business. I am bringing one of the tents along as a sample of what we will be weaving. It will mean retooling our looms and changing patterns to produce this new type of tent. So I am going to be busy for some time before going out again to secure more orders.

"I hope my uncle Saul is at home now. He was an even more avid scholar than I was. Since he felt called to a religious life, he was sent to Jerusalem to study under the great Jewish scholar Gamaliel. While there he became a member of the party of the Pharisees, and, I am told, is now one of their leading scholars and teachers.

"There! There!" shouted Jason. "You can see the city coming into sight now. Back of it is the waterfall where the snowmelt from the mountains makes its last plunge and spreads out into a small lake that we use for irrigation. The water is heavily laden with silt washed from the highlands above the falls, so a delta is building up quite rapidly between the lake and the Sea. It is on this ground that Tarsus is built and the fields around it are very productive."

"I begin to see why you are so excited. But where is your factory?"

"Factory? Well I never heard it called that before, but it is on the other side of town and not visible from here. I hope the ship will be in port for a few days so you can meet my family and have a tour of the workshop."

To Jason and Antonio's delight, the ship's captain announced that they would be in port for two or three days, so anyone who wanted to visit the city would be at leisure to do so.

As they left the ship Jason warned his friend to be careful not to fall into the river. "The water is frigid cold, since it has not had time to warm up since it left the snowfields on Mt. Taurus." He laughed as he continued:

"Once when one of the Caesars was visiting the city he plunged into the river for a swim. The water was so cold that he was immediately frozen stiff and could not swim nor cry out for help. Fortunately some of the natives of the city saw what had happened and launched a boat to quickly rescue him. It took a long time to warm him up before their fire before he could thank them and return to his ship."

The recounting of this tale reminded Jason to tell his friend of the time Cleopatra of Egypt brought Mark Anthony to Tarsus on her royal yacht. She had intended to find a luxurious hideaway where she could woo him and get him to join her as her husband and be the king of Egypt. But since they could not find any private, luxurious hotel, they had to remain on board her yacht all the time they were there.

When they arrived at the workshop Jason was delighted to show Antonio how the looms worked and to introduce him to the manager of the company. To his disappointment he did not find his Uncle Saul there. Since everyone was very busy, they recommended that the two friends go at once to Saul's home and talk to his wife Hannah[1] about his whereabouts and activities.

Jason was pensive all the way to Saul's house. There seemed to be some mystery afloat that he could not understand. As they approached Saul's home, his wife, Hannah, answered their greeting and rushed into Jason's arms as soon as she saw him. Jason, after greeting her affectionately, introduced her to his friend, Antonio, then asked quickly for his Uncle Saul.

"Didn't they tell you?" gushed Hannah enthusiastically, "Saul has decided to become a rabbi! Isn't that just wonderful?"

Chapter II
Saul Becomes a Pharisee

Jason was not surprised to find that his uncle had decided upon a religious career. He had always been a profound student of the Torah in the synagogue school and outdid all of his fellow Jewish lads in his devotion to Jehovah and his deep piety. Saul had always seemed more inclined toward a religious vocation than to tent making, although, since a rabbi did not live off his students, but had to furnish his own living, he had to have a profession of some kind to earn his living. Tent-making thus became Saul's means of livelihood.

Jason also learned that, since there was no rabbinical school in Tarsus, Saul had decided to go to Jerusalem and study under the great teacher Gamaliel. Hannah graciously offered to take her husband's place in the tent-making business while he studied in Jerusalem. Saul returned home as often as his study schedule allowed to spend time with Hannah and to secure more funds for his expenses. He was rising rapidly among the rabbis and it is rumored that he will soon become a member of the Sanhedrin.[1]

Wanting to visit with his uncle, and learn more about the rabbinical school, Jason asked for some time off to go to Jerusalem and visit with Saul. His request was quickly granted and in a few days he was walking the streets of Jerusalem searching for the school of Gamaliel.

He soon found directions to the school, and discovered that classes had been dismissed for the day. The students, however, had not yet gone home but were excitedly discussing the meaning of the lesson of the day. Searching from group to group Jason soon located his uncle and shouted: "Uncle Saul, Uncle Saul, I've been looking everywhere for you."

"Jason, my boy, what are you doing in Jerusalem?"

"I've been looking for you. When I found you were not at home I came here to find you and find out why you are here and not in Tarsus."

"Didn't they tell you I am studying to be a rabbi?"

"Yes, but I couldn't believe you were leaving our tent-making business. I have just come home with orders for army tents that will require full time work for all our labor force."

"I am glad for that, and I congratulate you on finding new markets to keep us going. But God has called me to a religious profession, and I will not be able to help you now. Hannah is taking my place in the business so they will not miss me."

"Well, I miss you. Let's go somewhere where we can talk about all this."

Saul knew of a good dining room where they could order a substantial meal and have leisure for a long, sincere conversation.

"You know, of course, Jason, that I have always been fascinated with the synagogue services, and the school held by our rabbi. Lately I have been restless while working at the shop. I had to come here where I could pursue my dream of being a rabbi some day."

"But why couldn't you do that while you work at the shop? We have a good rabbi at our synagogue who could teach you."

"He is a good rabbi, but he has taught me all he knows. But here we have great teachers who spend all their time in study and teaching. Haven't you heard of the great Gamaliel? He is the greatest teacher of our time and I am studying with him every day."

"What does he know that our rabbi doesn't?"

"Well, for instance, do you know the difference between Sadducees, Pharisees and Essenes? [2]

"No I don't, but what difference does that make?"

"It makes all the difference in the world because they have different beliefs about God and the Bible and how best to live a religious life. Maybe I had better explain this to you."

"Yes, do by all means."

"Well, in the first place, these parties arose after the Holy Scriptures[3] were written. You do know, of course, that after the time of the Old Testament, our people were in bondage and harassed by foreign countries—Babylon, Nineveh, Greece and Rome. But there was one short period where God's people gained their independence and had their own Jewish kings. This is now called the Macabbean (sometimes called the Hasmonean) period.

"During this time three political parties developed who had different approaches to governing the people. They were called the Sadducees, the Pharisees, and the Essenes. Gradually, the Sadducees became the leading political party. It was the party of the priests and Levites who dominated the government of the country, the Sanhedrin and the Temple priesthood.

"The Pharisees, seeing they were excluded from government affairs, began to concentrate on the religious life of the people, and developed an amazing number of rules and regulations to be obeyed by the people. The Essenes, disillusioned with all this rivalry and controversy, tended to withdraw from public life and live lives of deep piety. Sometimes they practiced this life style at home, and sometimes they retreated from society and formed religious societies in solitary places.

"Now that we do not have a government of our own, the Sadducees try to control our destiny by collaborating with the Romans, hoping to influence them to respect our faith and life. The Pharisees have become the religious party and deal with theology and practical religious living."

"Where do you stand amid all this confusion?" Jason questioned.

"There is no doubt in my mind," declared Saul emphatically, "I will be a Pharisee. They are only ones who really believe in God and the Holy Scriptures and they believe firmly in the resurrection of the body and a life after death with God."

Jason was not at all satisfied with his interview with his uncle Saul, but reluctantly returned to Tarsus to continue with his commitment to their tent-making business.

Chapter III
New Markets for Tent Makers

Feeling great loss at Saul's abandonment of the family and its thriving business, Jason returned home. He respected Saul's choice to become a rabbi, but found it hard to accept. He wasn't in Tarsus long, however, until he was again caught up in his efforts to expand the company by securing new orders for army tents.

Leaving Tarsus to look for new clients, he encountered a businessman who encouraged him to cross over into Macedonia to seek new customers. In Macedonia, he heard of Lydia of Thyatira and sought out her place of business. Getting right to the point, he asked, "What kind of cloth and manufactured goods do you deal with?"

After learning she carried mostly exotic fabrics dyed with a rare purple dye, he explained that he was a tent-maker and was actually at the moment expanding his family's business by making tents for the Roman Army.

"I am looking for distributors for our tents in Macedonia. Would you like to add these tents to your line of products?"

As they discussed the advantages and disadvantages of such an arrangement, Jason became conscious of a second person who had entered the room.

"I am glad Martha has arrived," explained Lydia. "She is my daughter, and has already demonstrated unusual acumen as a businesswoman. She handles the business end of our enterprise with unusual efficiency."

"I . . . am glad to meet you," stammered Jason. "I am . . . sure you are a great addition to the efficiency of this business," he continued as he stared into the beautiful, expressive eyes and smiling face of the young woman before him. Inwardly, he sighed with relief that he had avoided saying "a lovely addition to this business."

With great effort Jason tore himself away from the contemplation of the lovely young woman before him and turned to Lydia to continue the discussion of joining their two enterprises.

Before long they had arrived at an agreement satisfactory to all three of them. Lydia then invited Jason to join them in their evening meal and they all retired to the private living quarters of the establishment.

I stayed longer than I intended to, thought Jason as he very reluctantly withdrew from his overwhelmingly kind and gracious new friends and business partners. He had no way of knowing that Lydia was, at that moment cautioning her daughter about becoming too attracted to a new friend, especially one whom she would see only occasionally and at long intervals.

* * * * * *

So this is Rome, Jason thought. *When I finish the business at hand, I'll have to visit the famed areas of the imperial city.* He was walking through a business section inquiring about tent-making businesses. Here he discovered that there was a shop that was engaged in weaving tents. After a long search he located it and eagerly introduced himself.

"I am Jason of Tarsus. My family has a prosperous tent-making business. Recently we have turned to making army tents as the market for our shepherd tents has nearly dried up. I am now on a tour of army camps taking new orders. It was there that I was told of your shop, and have searched for you for the purpose of seeing if we can join together in this enterprise."

"Do you have any samples of the tents you are making?"

"Yes, I have," replied Jason, as he hurried out to secure one of the tents to show to his new friends. "This is one of the tents for the common soldiers. Of course the ones for officers are larger and more elaborate."

"I can see at once that our looms would not accommodate this weight of cloth and the size of the tents," said Aquila dubiously.

"I realize that," replied Jason. "We had to modify our looms to be able to weave these tents. I would be able to modify yours, if you will join in our plans. I believe the orders for tents like this will be limitless. If you were willing to join with us I am sure I could get all the orders we can fill."

The new friends spent the rest of the day making supply lists for Aquilla and his wife, Priscilla,[1] and planning how to modify their looms for their joint effort to fill the army's need for tents.

Chapter IV
Confrontation in Jerusalem

When the new partnership was up and running in Rome, Jason started for home, making sure to stop in Greece to see Martha before continuing on home.

He found that Lydia was completely opposed to his courtship of Martha, but that did not stop the two lovers from spending a long time together trying to figure out ways to convince Lydia that they were meant for each other. Finally, in frustration, Jason had to leave and continue his journey on to Tarsus.

Upon arriving, he went immediately to the house of Saul. He found a very disturbed Hannah who informed him that Saul was at home, but that he was living in seclusion and refused to see anyone.

"I am very worried about him. Something strange happened to him on a trip to Damascus. He was going there to arrest some people of the 'Way' which has sprung up. They proclaim that Jesus, who was crucified at the last Passover, is still living. They assert that he has been resurrected. Your uncle claimed that that is impossible and has been arresting those who are preaching that He is alive."

"But, I thought that Uncle Saul believed in the resurrection."

"I did too, and reminded him of that."

"What did he say?"

"He said that he does believe in a resurrection, but that will happen when God comes to earth in the last days—not now."

"Is that all he said about it?"

"He said that Jesus appeared to him on the road to Damascus—struck him down on the road and blinded him. He even called out to him: 'Saul, Saul, why do you persecute me?'"

"What did Uncle Saul say to that?"

"He said he cried out: 'Who are you, Lord?'"

"Don't tell me that the Lord answered him."

"He sure did. He said: 'I am JESUS whom you are persecuting. Now get up and go into the city, and you will be told what you must do.' "[1]

They both paused for a while, Jason deeply puzzled and concerned, and Hannah trying to control her deep fear.

"Let me see if I can get him to talk to me. Maybe he will talk to me. We have always been very close."

But the effort was a total failure. Saul adamantly refused to see or talk to him. Finally Jason was forced to leave in order to deliver some of the army tents and secure more orders.

* * * * * *

Anticipation filled Jason as he awoke to the sounds of the sea. This would be the last day of his return journey to Tarsus.

This trip had been most profitable. He had left his partners in Thyratira and Rome working steadily to fill the tent orders he had given them, and the additional orders he brought with him would keep the family looms in Tarsus humming for many weeks. But, as had always happened during the eleven years since his uncle Saul had become a believer in Jesus, the pleasure of coming home was tinged with depression.

With the docking of the ship, Jason set out, first of all, to Saul's house to see how he was. He was shocked to find Hannah in tears as she told him that a man named Barnabas had called at their home and had persuaded Saul to go to Antioch with him to minister to a mixed group of Jews and Greeks who had been persuaded to believe that Jesus was really the Jewish Messiah, but that his message was to Greeks as well as to Jews.

"How could that be?"

"Your uncle now believes that Jesus was God himself and that he had died on the cross for the sins of all mankind—not just the Jews. You know that Saul is a very eloquent man. Many people are now believing his new message, especially the Jewish Proselytes."

"I can't believe what you are saying."

"It is true though, and from what I hear, these people are being cast out of the synagogues. Your uncle and this Barnabas are organizing them into associations they call 'churches' where they meet to worship Jesus whom they call God. They even have a name for these fanatics—they are being called Christians (worshippers of Jesus the Christ)."

"This is worse than I could have imagined. I am going to Antioch as soon as I get my business done here. I am going to get to the bottom of this. I only hope I can talk some sense into Uncle Saul."

* * * * * *

"He was not there any longer!" Jason reported to Hannah, upon his return from Antioch. "Uncle Saul and this Barnabas were commissioned to go to Barnabas' home country of Cyprus to spread the 'Good News.' "

By now, Jason was furious. He had found traces of Saul and Barnabas in Cyprus, and then had lost track of them. Finally, he realized that he would have to give up his search for Saul for now and concentrate on the expansion of the family business. What he did not know was that Saul, while evangelizing the Roman governor of Cyprus, had become aware that it would be an important advantage to use his Roman name and citizenship while moving about in the Roman world. So from that time on he took the leadership of their evangelistic efforts and always used his Roman name, Paulus [Paul].

Since he seemed to have lost all contact with his uncle and Barnabas, Jason was forced to return to Tarsus to finish the tents he had contracted for from the Army and then deliver them to the army camps involved. This, as well as preparing and delivering new orders, kept him busy for many months.

Ready at last to make a canvass of the army camps in Asia Minor, he called on the captain of the army garrison in Tarsus, for directions and permission to visit these camps.

"I will be ascending the Cilician Gates route and then traveling westward, visiting the army camps that I find along the way," he informed the captain. He was well aware of the difficulty of the trip, both from narrow paths cut into the rock walls to bypass the places made dangerous by falling water, and because of the brigands that frequented the trail. But he was surprised when the captain firmly counseled him not to attempt the dangerous ascent through the Gates.

"But that is the shortest and best way to reach the camps I want to explore. If you will give me the names and locations of those camps, I will go at once and show them the tents we are making and take orders for more."

Again the captain advised against the plan, and finally told him plainly: "I am not only advising you, I will not allow you to make this trip. It is too risky and may very well end in tragedy."

Jason still argued with the captain and demanded permission to make the trip although he knew it would be dangerous.

Finally the captain relented to a degree. "I will be making an inspection trip to the army camps in the spring," he said. "If you will wait until then you may accompany me and my soldiers up the Gates and to the camps we have established in Asia Minor."

Although it was several months before the army's inspection trip, Jason at last realized that was the only way he would be able to reach the camps he desired to visit. Reluctantly he acceded and spent the winter months making more tents that he was sure he would be able to sell in the spring.

* * * * * *

At last the long-anticipated trip began. Even though he had heard many stories of the hardships of this ascent, he was surprised that, in several places where the foaming water tore at the rock walls on both sides, the dangerous path had to leave the bottom of the gulch to find footholds that had been cut in the solid rock walls as a path for the travelers.

There were also several caves in the rock walls. These gave rest and safety to travelers, but also provided hiding places for brigands who lay in wait for rich travelers and caravans.

The captain always stopped before passing any of these caves to give his scouts time to determine that there were no robbers hiding there. They were surprised not to encounter any difficulty until they were almost to the top of the long climb. The captain explained that it was early spring and that no rich caravans had yet arrived, so the brigands had not yet set up ambushes in the caves. They thought that they were going to reach the highlands above the gulch without any trouble when suddenly they heard the unmistakable sounds of battle just above them.

Since the path was wide enough at this point to allow the soldiers to charge three abreast, the captain quickly formed them for battle and ordered them to charge. As they rounded a corner in the trail, they came upon a large band of robbers battling with a caravan that had just started the descent. The bandits had already captured some of the heavily laden mules, stripping them of their cargo and pushing the screaming mules over the banks to death on the rocks below when the soldiers arrived. Shouting their battle cry, the soldiers charged. Seeing the soldiers in their rear and the courage of the caravan drivers, the robbers quickly dispersed, some of them seeking refuge in a large cave nearby where they had been lying in wait.

To his deep satisfaction, Jason was at last able to engage in the battle with the remaining robbers. He was shocked, however, that the captain ordered all the bandits to be put to death and their bodies thrown into the raging river.

"Why didn't you take the robbers prisoners instead of killing them all?" Jason asked.

"We don't have time nor soldiers enough to herd prisoners through this dangerous country," replied the captain tersely.

They hadn't proceeded very far north until they came to a well paved Roman highway. "Why did the Romans build such a fine road in this wilderness?" Jason asked.

"This is the Roman military highway built the length of Asia Minor and linking all the important towns in this part of the country with ports on the Aegean Sea. It not only allows the movement of troops easily and rapidly but also facilitates the movement of mail and government messengers."

"Are there many army camps along this highway?"

"Yes, in all the important towns. We will be coming to the first one at Antioch in Pisidia soon."

"See what a strategic location Antioch has?" the captain pointed out with pride to Jason, who was now his esteemed friend. "Notice how it is located on a low plateau some 50 to 100 feet above the plain. It rises abruptly from the Anthios River, [2] which makes it easily visible from the countryside and also easily defensible. You will be surprised to know that it also has a large and beautiful synagogue."

"You mean there are enough Jews here to have a synagogue?" [3]

"Oh, yes. There are thousands of Jews in the countryside and in the principal towns. They have become very prosperous merchants and are a valuable part of the populace. I have heard it said that there are many more Jews in Asia Minor, Greece, Italy and Spain than in Palestine. There are many of them even in Egypt and North Africa."

"Well, I have heard that many Jews live outside of Palestine, but I had no idea they were so numerous and wide-spread. I am going to try to find them as I travel around looking for army camps."

"I'm sorry. I didn't know you were interested in Jewish synagogues. All of the principal towns have them. We have already passed by at least three of them—in Derbe, Lystra and Iconium.

True to his word, Jason began looking for Jews wherever he went. Finding large and prosperous synagogues in nearly all the principal towns, he soon became aware that the synagogues were in turmoil. Little by little he discovered the reason: a popular and charismatic figure named Paulus was systematically visiting the synagogues and preaching a new message, saying that the Messiah had already come and declaring that the Good News of salvation was for all people—Gentiles as well as Jews. Of course most of the Jews rejected this doctrine, but some of them and many of the proselytes were leaving the synagogues and forming what they called "Christian churches."

Everywhere he went, Jason encountered the destruction of the true faith by this stranger who called himself Paulus. *That sounds a lot like the new doctrine that Uncle Saul and his companion Barnabas preached in Antioch of Syria and on Cyprus,* Jason thought with a sinking feeling. At first brushing the horrible implication aside as preposterous, he finally realized that he had to find out the truth, so he asked one of the adherents of the new faith: "Was this rabbi accompanied by a man named Barnabas?"

"No, I never heard the name Barnabas. He had a young assistant, though, by the name of Timothy. They tell me that he is from Lystra. His mother was a Jewess, but his father was not."

Deeply worried about what was happening to the synagogues in this part of the world, Jason finally accosted his friend, the army captain: "Why don't you arrest this man and put a stop to his depredations?"

"It's out of our hands. Don't you realize that this is a quarrel among Jewish rabbis about religious doctrine? We can only deal with civil matters which affect the Roman government. If anything is done about him, it will be by you Jews giving him a religious trial and sentencing him to whatever fate you think he deserves."

"But we cannot crucify anyone."

"No, but you could stone him to death. In fact they tried to do that at Lystra." [4]

"Tried to? What happened?"

"They stoned him, alright. When he collapsed, they drug him out of the city and left him by the roadside for dead. It seems he was only unconscious, because when his friends arrived to carry him into the city for burial, they found he was still breathing. So they revived him. As soon as he could walk they escorted him out of the city, and he continued his preaching in other towns."

"I'm going to hunt for him until I find him and then make sure he doesn't keep on deceiving the people," vowed Jason, with deep emotion.

"Well, our tour is over. We will be heading back to Tarsus tomorrow, so you'll have to do that some other time," replied the captain.

After a short pause, Jason replied: "I think I will stay for a while. I want to visit a good friend in Thyatira before I go home, and then I will make a stop in Ephesus on my way back home. I think I will be able to find a ship sailing from Ephesus to Tarsus."

"I'll be sorry to lose your company. I have really enjoyed having you with us on this tour."

"I'll be sorry too, but hopefully we can meet again in Tarsus."

Jason was anxious to go on to Macedonia to see Martha, but decided to curb his impatience and visit Ephesus first. His journey across Mysia led naturally down the course of the river Rhyndacos[5] to Ephesus, the city of the great goddess Diana, also known as Artemis. Ephesus had formerly been the principal port city of eastern Asia Minor, but the river had silted in until boats could no longer reach its wharves. So the city fathers had had to relocate the city farther upstream and build makeshift wharves on one of the arms of the delta now formed by the river. From here a road was built beside the river to reach Ephesus.

As Jason searched in vain for the famed temple of Diana of the Ephesians, he encountered an old man, leaning on a crutch, also seeming to be searching for something.

"Hello, friend. What are you searching for?" inquired Jason.

"I am looking for the ruins of the temple of the great Diana and the statue that fell down from heaven."

"Have you never seen them then?"

"No, but my father described them well for me. He says they are in ruins now, but when he was a lad the statute stood tall and beautiful before a temple that was one of the Seven Wonders of the Ancient World. The temple was 400 ft. long and 220 feet wide. It was surrounded by Ionic pillars, sixty feet high.[6]

Together they searched until at last they found the famous statue of Diana. It stood before the ruins of the famous temple that was now falling into decay. Much of the building had already fallen down. Even some of the beautiful pillars were lying prone on the grassy hillside.

"So this is the statue that caused the famous riot in Ephesus,"[7] mused Jason.

"Don't tell me you have heard of that riot."

"Yes, I have heard all about it and would like to know more."

"Well, I don't think there is any more to tell. The city clerk dismissed all charges since it was a religious quarrel among Jews and was not anything that he had jurisdiction over."[8]

"That's what I keep hearing," Jason commented with frustration. "Somehow, these Christian trouble-makers need to be stopped."

* * * * * *

Now Jason was free to make his long desired trip to see his beloved Martha. He told himself that this time he would not listen to her mother's objections, but would insist on setting a date for the wedding.

He had never seen Martha so alive and animated. She ran to him with her arms open wide and engulfed him with a warm embrace.

"My, I have never seen you so loving and so animated," Jason cried.

"Oh, darling, I have such good news for you. We have had a guest in our house who has taught us new joy and faith in God. He showed us that Jesus really was God himself in human flesh and that he died for our sins and for the sins of the whole world."[9]

"No, no, no, my dear. You have been deluded. Who is this man you speak of?"

"His name is Paulus."

"Paulus! That is the man I have been searching for. He has gone all over Asia Minor and has wrecked synagogues everywhere he has gone. He has led many astray and is establishing 'churches' everywhere made up of Jews and Greeks together. When I find him, I will silence him forever."

"Oh, no, Jason, he truly is a man of God. You must believe him."

Late that night Jason left the home of Lydia and Martha in despair. He had not been able to convince them of his fears about Paulus, and now realized that Martha was lost to him forever, for he could not accept Paulus' teachings. What had been anger and frustration was now fierce hatred for Paulus. He was determined in his desire to destroy him and his teachings.

Realizing that he had come to a dead end in his search for his uncle Saul, and that he was now engaged in a search for Paulus, Jason reluctantly turned his steps back to Tarsus. On the way, considering the fact it had been a long time since he had celebrated the Passover in Jerusalem, he decided to make a stop there to fulfill this obligation. Possibly he might find some more traces of his uncle or Paulus while there.

* * * * * *

No one seemed to have heard of Saul, but he did learn that the renegade Paulus was reported to be in Jerusalem, so he began a careful search for him. He soon found out that there were radical groups of Jews who were actively searching for him also. Joining one of them, Jason was at first shocked to realize the deep hatred they held for Paulus and their plans to kill him as soon as they found him. He had to admit, though, that he had harbored the same feelings, and yes, the same purpose.

At last came the electrifying news—"He is in the Temple with some of his Greek friends!"

Jason charged into the Temple with his fanatical friends and assisted them in grabbing the surprised Jew who was busy cleansing himself for the celebration of the Passover. Even though he had not gotten a look at his face, Jason helped to drag the offending heretic out of the Temple and joined them as they began to beat and stone him.

In the Roman fort (the Praetorium) just across the street the Roman lookout cried: "Riot in the Temple!"

Immediately a squad of soldiers, held in readiness for just such an emergency, burst out of the fort and, charging into the melee, rescued the unfortunate Jew from his enemies who were bent on killing him. The angry crowd was so threatening and angry that the soldiers had to pick up the hapless victim and carry him bodily across the street and up the steps into the fort. Furious at losing their chance to kill Paulus, the conspirators at once put their heads together and decided to request the commander to take Paulus to the Sanhedrin the following day. They would lie in wait and kill him on the way.

While Jason's band was regrouping, Paulus, on his way up the steps of the fort called to the commander of the troops for permission to address the angry crowd. Surprisingly, the commander assented and Saul (Paulus) began his defense in the Hebrew language.

"Brothers and fathers, listen now to my defense. . . I am a Jew, born in Tarsus of Cilicia, but brought up in this city. Under Gamaliel I was thoroughly trained in the law of our fathers and was just as zealous for God as any of you are today.

I persecuted the followers of this Way to their death, arresting both men and women and throwing them into prison, as also the high priest and all the Council can testify. I even obtained letters from them to their brothers in Damascus, and went there to bring these people as prisoners to Jerusalem to be punished.

"About noon as I came near Damascus, suddenly a bright light from heaven flashed around me. I fell to the ground and heard a voice say to me, 'Saul! Saul! Why do you persecute me?'

" 'Who are you, Lord?' I asked.

" 'I am Jesus of Nazareth, whom you are persecuting,' he replied. . . 'What shall I do Lord?' I asked.

" 'Get up,' the Lord said, 'and go into Damascus. There you will be told all that you have been assigned to do.'[10]

"When I returned to Jerusalem the Jews would not listen to my message. They set about to harm me, but the Lord was with me and instructed me: 'Go, I will send you far away to the Gentiles.' "[11]

Jason, engrossed in the hurried plotting of his group, had missed the first part of Paulus' speech to the crowd on the steps of the fort. Now as he approached and heard what Paulus was saying, he thought to himself: "This man is really a fraud; he has stolen my uncle's experience and is trying to justify himself by claiming it is about him." But as the narrative proceeded, he had to admit that the man was talking about a real experience he had had. At this point he pressed closer so he could see the face of the speaker. It was then that he realized that at last he had found his long-lost uncle Saul. But this raised a new dilemma in his mind. Who and where was Paulus?

Jason wandered the streets of Jerusalem for what seemed like hours struggling with his doubts and his loyalties. Finally he decided that the only way to solve them was to have an interview with Saul. So he visited the fort and asked to see the prisoner. He was finally able to convince them of his honesty and was conducted to the cell where Saul was confined.

Saul was surprised to receive a visitor in his cell, but he recognized him immediately and exclaimed: "Jason, Jason. Oh, I am so glad to see you! But how did you know I was here?"

"I heard you speaking on the steps of the Praetorium. I was with the fanatics who were trying to kill you because they thought you were that renegade Jew Paulus. I didn't realize it was you and that they were mistaken. I actually was trying to help them kill you," he sobbed. "Now you are in greater danger than ever, because they are going to ask the commander to bring you to the Sanhedrin tomorrow so they can question you and find out what you really believe. Don't go, for they are preparing to ambush you and kill you before you reach the Sanhedrin."

"Jason, Jason, please calm down and listen to me. You know that we both are Roman citizens as well as Jews. I also have a Roman name—Paulus (Paul). Since I am working outside of Palestine most of the time, I use my Roman name. It gives me access to all the privileges and rights of a Roman citizen. I can pass from one province to another without needing a passport and have free access to Roman roads, the Roman postal system, and to Roman courts to protect me from fanatical Jews like you have been describing."

"But, Uncle Saul," Jason insisted, "This Paulus we have been searching for is destroying synagogues wherever he goes."

"No, no, no. I go to the synagogues wherever I am and preach to them the good news that the Messiah has come and is even now reigning in the hearts of the faithful. Many of them—especially the God Fearers—believe the truth and accept Jesus as their Messiah. But the rulers of the synagogues usually get so angry that they throw us out. It is only then that I gather the faithful ones together and provide a place and time where they can meet to worship. They always choose leaders for the new band just as the Jews do in the synagogues."

Chapter V
Paulus in Prison in Caesarea

Suddenly Jason remembered the urgency of his uncle's position. "I really came to see you at this time to tell you that the radical band I was a member of is going to request that you be sent back to the Sanhedrin tomorrow. You must not go," he repeated, "for they have prepared an ambush and have sworn to kill you when you leave the fort."

"Then we must get word to the captain at once. Call the guard so I can give him this information."

When Jason had called the guard, Paulus carefully explained to him the situation and requested that he inform the captain. He at once ordered Jason to accompany him to the captain's office. "This nephew of the prisoner Paulus has some urgent information for you," he announced.

Taking him aside, the captain asked: "What is this important information you have for me?"

"I have heard a band of Jewish patriots plot to ask you to send Paulus to the Sanhedrin so they can question him about his teachings tomorrow. Do not do so, for they will be lying in wait to assassinate him."[1]

"How do you know that these assassins will be waiting for him?"

"I was a member of one of those groups until I saw Paulus and recognized him as my uncle. I have to prevent them from killing him."

After carefully examining Jason's story, the captain was finally convinced that Paulus really was in danger from these bands of zealots, so he announced: "I will transfer him tonight to Caesarea. Will you go along to attend to his care and safety?"

"I certainly will, and gladly."

As soon as it was dark, the commander assembled a squad of cavalry and foot soldiers to escort Paulus and Jason to Caesarea. They descended as far as Antipatris on the Plain of Sharon that night.

This does appear to be fertile land, Jason thought to himself, as they set out again the next day. *I can believe that this plain produces as many as three crops in one year.* The cavalry had turned back to Jerusalem that morning, leaving Paulus and Jason to be escorted the rest of the way to Caesarea by the foot soldiers.

Back in Jerusalem, the priests were furious. Having visited the Praetorium and found out that Paulus had already been sent to Caesarea, they were left with no better option than to accompany the commander when he returned to Caesarea for a trial before the governor, Felix. This they did, after the Passover.

* * * * * *

"Well, Uncle," Jason said heavily, "I believe I've discovered why you were not acquitted at your trial before Felix. I have just returned from a consultation with him. The governor informed me that you will be allowed to live in your own house (under guard), but that you will have to pay for you own expenses. He also broadly hinted that your complete release could be granted depending on how much you could contribute to Felix for this purpose."

"I'm not surprised," Paulus replied slowly, already deep in thought about this new circumstance. After a moment he continued, "Even if I believed in resorting to bribery for my release, I would not want to take that course. I would rather have my name cleared of these spurious charges. And I'm sure that with a proper defense, Felix will eventually acquit me."

"Have you forgotten the most obvious reason for not being released right now, Uncle?" Jason exclaimed. "Your assassins will still be waiting for you to leave Roman custody."

"True. My course of action must be to reside here and petition Felix for a new trial."

"That brings up another consideration—funds for your expenses while awaiting trial. It appears that I need to return to Tarsus. I shall approach the family about this matter."

* * * * * *

Back in Tarsus, Jason was surprised to find that news of Saul's beating and arrest had reached Tarsus and Hannah was worried and upset about her husband. Jason was able to calm her fears, but took advantage of her worries to plead for funds for Saul's maintenance while awaiting further trial.

At first she was completely opposed to releasing any funds, but Jason was at last able to overcome her reluctance by relating his own doubts and how he had finally come to realize that Saul was completely sincere and persuaded that Jesus was indeed risen from the dead and that he was in fact the Christ as he claimed. Relenting at last, Hannah gave Jason funds for her husband's maintenance but adamantly refused to bribe Felix for his release.

* * * * * *

Now that Paulus was installed in his own house and had funds for his maintenance, Jason at last felt free to leave him for a while to care for his own business of tent making which had been on hold while he ministered to his uncle.

His first trip included a stop at the home of Lydia and Martha. He was anxious to make amends for his harsh words concerning Paulus to Martha at their last meeting. He was surprised to find only Lydia at home.

"Where is Martha? I want to apologize for my harsh words about Paulus on my last visit here. I realize now that he is my uncle Saul and that he really has seen the Christ and is preaching the truth."

"I am glad that you now know the truth about Paulus. But Martha is no longer here. She was convinced that she could no longer hope to marry you, so when one of her former admirers called to renew his suit for her hand, she accepted his offer. They are now married and are living at the university where her husband is a professor."

Stunned and disappointed, Jason left immediately and finished his business trip as soon as possible so he could return to Caesarea and renew his relationship with his uncle.

He still found it difficult to believe all the new ideas Paulus was preaching and wanted more time to talk with him about them. It soon became apparent that Felix was not going to release Paulus any time soon, so Jason resumed his business of finding new outlets for tents among the many Army camps in new areas.

One of these trips took him as far west as Spain. He was amazed to find so many Jews in this frontier province of Rome, and to find that so many of them were important personages in the province and even advisors to the governor of Spain. The one he was the most impressed with was Maimonides. He spent many days in conference with him not just about business matters, but about the new Christian faith that had already penetrated Spain.

He was also impressed with the youngest daughter of Maimonides whose name was Maria. She was not only beautiful but well educated, and acted as the business manager of her father's estate. It was with reluctance that Jason finally finished his business with Maimonides and began his trip back to Tarsus and Caesarea.

* * * * * *

Back in Caesarea, Jason found that a new governor had replaced Felix. However, Felix had left Paulus in custody and turned him over to the new governor, Festus, apparently to appease the Jews.

Jason continued to care for the needs of Paulus by frequent visits and also by securing more funds for his maintenance from Hannah, while also traveling as the recruiter of new orders for their tent making business.

As the months and years rolled by, Paulus finally realized that his only opportunity for release would be to appeal his case to Caesar,[2] which he was able to do since he was not only a Jew but also a Roman citizen. So when he was again called to trial by Festus he made that appeal. Festus had no choice but to honor his appeal, but still held him in custody until he could determine what charges were valid against him, and then to secure passage for him on a ship to Rome under custody.

CHAPTER VI
SHIPWRECK

Jason and Paulus soon found that the waiting was not over yet. Paulus had to be sent to Rome on a ship under guard by Roman soldiers. Since the Roman army did not have ships of their own—except perhaps warships—there was nothing to do but wait for a commercial ship with room for the prisoner and his party. They would also be responsible for their food and maintenance while on the trip. So Jason had to make a quick trip to Tarsus to secure more funds from Hannah.

Finally a ship docked at Caesarea heading north for Sidon. Paulus, Jason and their party were placed on board under the guard of a centurion named Julius and his company of soldiers who were escorting several other prisoners to Rome.[1] They sailed north along the coast as far as Sidon, where Paulus and his party were allowed to go ashore to visit his friends so that they might provide for their needs.

They continued to sail northward until they reached the southern shores of Asia Minor. Now, turning west, they sailed along the coast as far as Myra in Lycia. Here they discovered an Alexandrian ship, carrying a full load of corn for Italy.[2] The ship captain and the owner of the cargo of grain were anxious to sail immediately for Rome. As the season was far advanced, and no other ship would be able to sail these seas once the fall storms commenced, their cargo of corn would sell at an excellent price.

Even so, they dared not sail west immediately, since the Aegean Sea at this point was full of small islands and uncertain currents. So they sailed at once to the south until they came to the island of Crete, then turned west again, sailing along the south side of this island until they came to a small port named Fair Havens.

Here at last, all the passengers on board began to clamor for the ship to anchor and stay until spring. Paulus, speaking with the authority of one who had sailed these seas before, addressed the ship owners and the Roman centurion as they stood on deck discussing their options: "Men, I can see that our voyage is going to be disastrous and bring great loss to ship and cargo, and to our own lives also."[3]

Despite these warnings, the owners of the ship and cargo persuaded the centurion that, since Fair Havens was a small port and did not offer good places for lodging and recreation, they should sail on as far as the city of Phoenix before stopping for the winter.[4]

When a favorable breeze arose they left Fair Havens and set sail for Phoenix. Before long, a wind of hurricane force, called The Northeastern (Euroclydon)[5] came roaring out of the North. The ship was caught by the violent wind and all the sails and tackle blown away. They scarcely could save the life boat, which they finally were able to hoist aboard. Fearing they would be blown on the sand bars of Syrtis Major and destroyed, as many other ships had been, they threw overboard all the remaining tackle and some of the cargo, wrapped the hull with strong ropes, threw out a sea anchor, and let the ship be driven. After many days they gave up all hope of being saved.

At that point in this harrowing experience, Paulus called the crew and passengers together and declared:

> "Men, you should have taken my advice not to sail from Crete; then you would have spared yourselves this damage and loss. But now I urge you to keep up your courage, because not one of you will be lost; only the ship will be destroyed. Last night an angel of God whose I am and whom I serve stood beside me and said, 'Do not be afraid, Paul. You must stand trial before Caesar and God has graciously given you the lives of all who sail with you.' So keep up your courage, men, for I have faith in God that it will happen just as he told me. Nevertheless, we must run aground on some island."[6]

After two weeks of being driven by hurricane winds, the sailors sensed that they were approaching land. Soundings proved it to be true, so they cast an anchor from the stern and waited for daylight. By first light they saw what proved to be a small island dead ahead. By maneuvering carefully, they headed the ship toward a shallow bay, but struck a sandbar quite some distance from the shore. Paulus again encouraged them to abandon the ship, which was breaking up, and either swim or float on pieces of the ship in order to reach the shore.[7]

"Look, there is a fire over here," shouted Jason as they neared the shore.

"Sure enough, there is," replied Paulus. "Let's carry some wood to add to the flames," he continued as he bent over to gather an armload of branches.

"Look out! There is a viper in that bundle of wood," Jason warned as he saw his uncle toss it on the fire.

The viper, feeling the heat of the flames, bit into Paulus' hand, but he simply shook it off into the fire.

The natives of the island, seeing the viper bite Paulus' hand began to shout among themselves: "This man must be a vile criminal. He has escaped the sea, but the gods will not let him live. . . . he will surely swell up and drop dead any moment now." But as Paulus continued to replenish the fire, they decided he must be a god.[8]

As the rescued sailors and passengers warmed themselves at the fire they asked their benefactors: "Why did you build this fire here on such a stormy day?"

"Ships are often wrecked on this shore during the winter time. We keep a lookout posted to watch for them during the storms."

When the castaways had dried their clothes and warmed themselves, they were conducted to a nearby estate owned by the chief official of the island, where they were treated royally and furnished shelter as they waited for the storm to blow itself out. While there, they learned that the chief official's father was ill. Paulus asked to see him and, after praying for him, placed his hands on him, and he was healed.

When this was noised abroad, the rest of the sick on the island sought out Paulus and were healed as he prayed and laid his hands on them.[9]

After about three months on the island, they boarded an Alexandrian ship that had wintered on the island and continued their journey to Rome. The ship stopped briefly at Syracuse on the island of Sicily and then proceeded on to Rhegium and Puteoli and finally arrived at Three Taverns on the Appian Way—the principal highway to Rome. Here they left the ship and were able to contact the Christian community in that city. Accompanied by many of these new friends, and rejoicing that the hardships of the journey were over, their progress on into the capital city of Rome was a triumphal procession.[10]

CHAPTER VII
CAPTIVITY AND TRIAL IN ROME

Paulus was dismayed to learn that he would have to wait at least two years before he could present his case to Caesar.[1] He was encouraged somewhat when Jason was able to secure a comfortable house for him and his companions. It was situated on a lot with considerable land enclosed in front of the house. In that area he could address the friends and guests that he now decided to invite to his "residence."

Three days later he called Jason to his side. "I want you to go through the city and invite the leaders of the synagogues to meet me here."

"Don't you mean the leaders of the Christian churches?"

"No, no. I want to meet the leaders of the synagogues first to find out if they will oppose me when I go to trial."

"Alright, I will summon them at once."

On the appointed day, they began to arrive. Paulus and Jason greeted them cordially. As soon as they all had assembled, Paulus stepped forward and addressed them: "Friends and fellow Jews, I have invited you here so we could become acquainted and to explain to you why I am here.

"As you probably know by now, I am a Jew of Tarsus. But because of the policy of granting Roman citizenship to the artisans of cities like Tarsus, I am also a Roman citizen. I am also a Pharisee and a member of the Sanhedrin. In this capacity I engaged in rounding up and arresting the members of the sect which is now known as 'The Way'. In one of my trips to Damascus to arrest more of these heretics, I met Jesus himself. He is now alive and has sent me to preach salvation to Greeks as well as Jews.

"In my last trip to Jerusalem to celebrate the Passover, I was attacked by a group of fanatics, who falsely accused me of taking Greeks into the Temple. They tried to kill me, but the Roman commander rescued me from their hands. I was sent to Caesarea to protect me from the mob who had vowed to kill me. After three years, I was forced to appeal my case to Caesar to avoid being handed over to the Jews who were waiting for a chance to kill me. Now I have arrived here, and I need to know if you will join my accusers or will assist in my defense."

After a discussion among the synagogue rulers, one of them replied to Paulus: "We have heard about this 'Way' and know that everywhere it is spoken against, but we would like to hear from you what it is all about."

They had many questions and Paulus answered all of them by citing proofs from the Holy Scriptures of the Old Testament. Some of them were impressed, and a few were inclined to believe Paulus, but the rest refused to admit to the validity of Paulus' arguments. As the day wore on some of the leaders began to leave. At last Paulus dismissed the rest of them, after giving them a hearty invitation to return, in a group or as individuals, for further discussions. [2]

When they had all left, Paulus turned to Jason. "I am disappointed that they were not more open to the truth, but at least we will not have to worry that they will complicate the trial with their opposition. Now you can invite the Christian leaders—better yet, invite everyone in the churches. I would like to get acquainted with all of them and assure them I am willing to meet with them any time whether they hold a position of leadership or not."

"I don't know how many churches there are in Rome yet, but I think you will be surprised at how many there are. I have been thinking about Aunt Hannah. I don't know if she knew we were shipwrecked or not, but she must be worried that she has not heard from us for so long. We will soon need more funds as well. Why don't you write her a letter that I can take to her when go I to secure more funds."

"That is a good plan. I will get started on the letter at once, while you locate the churches here in Rome. Take Luke or one of the other evangelists with you so they can issue our invitations after you are gone."

The next days were busy ones for Jason as he located the churches in Rome and introduced Paulus' other helpers to them, so they would have confidence in them and accept their invitations when the time came. He was surprised and delighted at the number of churches and their eager reception of his helpers. Most of them wanted to come at once, so a schedule had to be worked out so they would all be able to come soon.

It was a happy day for Jason, and a nostalgic one for Paulus, when he was at last able to leave Rome and head for Tarsus. The trip took relatively little time as he was able to contact ships on the busy sea lanes from Rome to Palestine and Egypt.

When he arrived in Tarsus, Jason went straight to the house of his uncle Saul. As he knocked on the door he shouted: "Aunt Hannah! Aunt Hannah!"

Jason heard running footsteps and then the door burst open. For a few seconds Hannah stood transfixed as she searched the face of her caller, and then she threw herself into his arms shouting: "Jason, Jason, where is my husband, Saul?"

"Never fear, he is fine, but he is still a prisoner. We finally arrived in Rome and he has been arraigned for his trial. It will be a long wait, I fear, for there are many others before him, but he is still confident that he will be acquitted. Here, I have brought you a letter from him."

"Come in. Come in. Make yourself comfortable while I read his letter. Then we can talk."

Jason closed his eyes as he sat quietly waiting for Hannah to read and reread the letter. Finally she was able to control her weeping long enough to say: "I can't believe what you have been through. It was even worse than I imagined. I was sure you had been lost."

"I was sure we were lost more than once, but Uncle Saul never lost hope. He was in constant touch with God and kept reassuring us that none of us would be lost. It was unreal how we all reached shore while the ship was torn to pieces by the waves."

"How long were you marooned on this island?"

"We were there all winter. When the weather turned favorable in the spring we were able to leave on a ship that had reached the island before the severe weather started and had wisely stayed in port until spring. They took us to Italy and up the coast as far as a village called 'Three Taverns.' There we were able to visit with the Christians before going on. Some of them went with us along the Appian Way until we were met by other Christians who had come from Rome to meet us. From there it was more like a triumphal procession on into the city."

"Where is Saul now? It doesn't sound like he is in prison."

"Since it will be at least two years until his trial begins, he has been allowed to live in a rented house with only one soldier to guard him. We found a house with several rooms and a large fenced-in yard. Uncle Saul has already called in the governors of the synagogues in Rome and is now inviting the Christian churches, one at a time, to come for worship and consultation. Since I needed to come to you to secure funds for the rent of this excellent property and his other expenses, I suggested he write you this letter. You should have seen him labor over it with tears in his eyes and frequent pauses for prayer and praise."

"You can be sure that the first thing he will do when he is acquitted will be to come here to see you. He has missed you so much and often bemoans the fact that you have had to be separated all of these years."

"Oh, forgive me Jason. I can see you are tired from your long trip. Let me get you a good meal; then you must go to bed. I will spend the night thanking God for protecting us all and thinking up questions to ask you tomorrow."

After a delicious and satisfying meal, Jason appreciated the good bed he was shown, and was asleep almost before he fell into bed. As she predicted, Hannah scarcely slept at all. She was so full of gratitude to God and so busy writing down questions she had long wanted answered.

The next morning Jason awoke to the wonderful aroma of his favorite breakfast. After satisfying his hunger he spent the whole morning trying to answer as many of Hannah's questions as he could. It seemed unreal to see how interested she had become in her husband's success and his clear explanations of scriptures she had often read, but not understood. Finally he had to break away in order to go to the shop and report his new orders which were not as abundant as he wished because of so much time spent with the care of Paulus.

After hours of serious discussion of his position with the company, at last Jason replied: "You are right, I have not been able to give full attention to my job, and I cannot see how I will able to do any better in the near future because of my dedication to Paulus and his cause. Can we not give my job to someone else? I would be able to train him in the next few months while Uncle Saul is waiting for trial. Then he could take over the job completely."

"But you seem so sure that Saul will be acquitted."

"Yes I am. And if so then I want to be able to give myself entirely to assist him in his work. If he is not acquitted, then I am prepared to take over his work myself."

There was a long silence in the room. Jason had been feeling this conviction for some time, but it was the first time he had declared it even to himself. His employers (all relatives) seemed to be in a state of shock, some of them with tears in their eyes.

Finally the patriarch of the family spoke. "Are you sure this is what you want? How will you support yourself if you are left alone?"

"I don't know. I might do as Uncle Saul has done for years—do some tent making in the evenings, or take a few orders now and then when I am near an army camp. Of one thing I am sure. God is calling me to this and I cannot turn away from His calling. I know He will care for me if I am in His will."

"You seem to be so sure of this. Have you been thinking of who could take your place in the company?"

"Yes, I have been thinking about my cousin Lucius.[3] He has been associated with Saul in some of his work, and I believe he has what it takes to carry on my work."

"How soon will you be returning to Rome?"

"I should get back soon, but I could stay two or three days if you wish."

"Then let us consider your offer. Come back in two days for our answer."

It was a solemn Jason that returned to Hannah's home that evening. She was deeply concerned and finally asked: "What happened, Jason?"

"I resigned my position with the company."

"Don't tell me they accepted."

"They asked me to come back the day after tomorrow for their answer."

Of course, Jason spent the evening explaining to Hannah his feelings and the discussion with his peers. She was astounded, but was more inclined to see and appreciate Jason's decision than his employers. They closed the day with sincere prayers for guidance and retired for the night.

The next day was one of severe trial for Jason, but when it was over he was more certain than ever that he had made the right decision. So the next morning he made his way confidently to the office.

Again it was the patriarch of the family who spoke: "We can see that you are still certain that you must resign from the company. Do you have any idea how to contact Lucius?"

"The last I heard he was in Rome, so if he is not still there, I would think I could find out from someone there where he is," replied Jason.

"Very well, then! We certainly are sad to lose you and your expertise from the company, but we admire your devotion to God and his cause. We accept your resignation, with regret, but wish you every success in your new career." Then picking up a letter, he handed it to Jason, saying: "This is for Lucius. It is his appointment to take your place along with an explanation that you will be training him for the job and introducing him to his territory."

Jason was overcome for a few moments, but was finally able to express his sincere thanks to all of them for their understanding and friendship.

"There is one thing more. We have been strongly opposed to this new Christian movement, but have come to believe that it is from God. So we want to have a small part in its success. We are happy to offer you a 'pension' for the work you have done for us so well, hoping it will contribute to your well being and success. Please accept it with our love and good will."

Jason could not hold back the tears that came as he embraced each one of his dear relatives and friends as he tried to express his love and appreciation for their understanding and help. He hurried back to Hannah to tell her of his extreme good fortune and the backing the company was giving to his cause.

Jason quickly gathered together the finished tents and took them with him when he left. Delivering them would be a good excuse for taking Lucius on a tour of Asia Minor and introducing him to their clients.

* * * * * *

He was distressed to find Paulus quite disconsolate. The wait for his trial seemed endless, and now the long absence of his trusted nephew had added to his discouragement. All of this vanished into thin air, though, at the sight of his beloved assistant and his eager shout: "Uncle Saul, I have resigned from my position with our tent-making company and am now free to join you permanently in spreading the 'Good News.'"

"But, how will you support yourself, and how will we get funds from Hannah for my support?"

"That has already been taken care of. The company has completely changed its attitude toward our work. They now want to aid in our efforts, so they will be sending me a small 'pension' each month. Along with that, Aunt Hannah will also send you an allotment from her funds. The only condition to all this is that Aunt Hannah insists that the first thing you do when the trial is over is to come and see her!"

Jason was not prepared for the flood of tears that poured down the cheeks of the great Apostle as Jason delivered Hannah's ultimatum. "Oh, how I have missed my beloved wife. Sometimes I have been afraid she would think that I don't love her anymore, and now I realize she has longed for me as I have for her."

"Why don't you write her a letter now? I know she would greatly love to hear from you."

"I'll do that right now! But I don't think I have any empty scrolls. Will you get me some? Get the very best. I want her to see how much I appreciate her."

Paulus spent several days as he outlined his many activities since he had been able to see his wife. Interspersed with these details he constantly reiterated his declaration of love and affection for her and promised to visit her as soon as he was released. Since he knew that Jason planned a trip through Asia Minor with Lucius, he also wrote letters to some of the congregations of Christians there—Ephesus, Colosse, and others.

* * * * * *

Jason was frustrated at first in his search for Lucius, but finally located a Christian congregation that knew of him. They indicated that he had gone to Libya, in North Africa. Here Jason found his cousin and quickly returned to Rome with him.

Jason's enthusiasm, as he outlined his work for him, quickly overcame any reluctance Lucius had felt at first, and they spent many hours discussing the importance and possibilities of the tent-making enterprise. Paulus was relieved of his concerns about the wisdom of Jason's change in occupation, and enthusiastically approved of the plans they had made for their excursion together to Asia Minor.

"I have letters ready for you to take to Ephesus, Colosse and Philippi. I have two more ready also—to Philemon and Timothy."

"We will be glad to take the ones to Ephesus and Colosse, but will have to send the one to Philippi by army mail courier, since we will not be going there on this trip. We will also see Philemon, but I am not sure where Timothy is now. We will either find him or mail it to him, though."

Then, turning to Lucius, Jason said: "I think it would be well for us to pitch and take down one of these tents, so you will know how to handle them and show the soldiers how to manage them when they are delivered."

As it turned out, it took several days of pitching and dismantling tents before Lucius felt competent to do it well by himself and teach the soldiers how to do it. Then, after securing a cart to haul the tents and oxen to draw it, they were on their way.

* * * * * *

After several deliveries to army camps, Lucius approached Jason with a smile on his face. "I really feel now that I can take care of the tent business and securing new orders, and that you can now devote your time to the churches."

Jason's faced beamed as he placed his hand on Lucius' shoulder. "I am sure you are ready now and will do a good job, but I would still like for you to accompany me when we visit the churches and add your testimony to mine as we speak of God's goodness and His plan for saving the world."

Before starting the journey back to Rome, the two evangelists decided it would be better for Lucius to continue on to Tarsus so that he could deliver the new orders he had taken, secure the tents already being made, and deliver them before returning to Rome to report to Paulus.

* * * * * *

"Where is Lucius?" Paulus cried, enthusiastically welcoming Jason back to Rome. "Don't tell me he has abandoned us."

"No, no, nothing like that. After working on a few deliveries, he informed me he could handle it by himself, so I could devote all my time to visiting the churches and instructing them. I agreed with him, but insisted that he also attend the churches with me whenever he could. He has done so well encouraging them with his enthusiastic testimonies. He has now proceeded on to Tarsus to deliver the new orders he has been taking and to gather up any tents ready for delivery and take them to the camps on his way back here. You will be gratified when you see how he has matured and taken on his new responsibilities."

A few days later, Jason burst into Paulus' house with a shout: "Your trial is scheduled for next week. I have just talked to the clerk of the court and he says that there are only five trials ahead of us now, and the outcome of all of them seems to be clear cut so we can count on being called next week. Let's go over our case once more, so we will be confident of the outcome."

After deciding on the wording of their defense, Jason suggested that they write it out so that there would be no mistakes and present a copy to the clerk of the court and to Caesar himself at the time of the trial. Then Paulus would read from his copy when called upon to testify.

The remaining days were spent in prayer and supplication to God for his direction and help in the presentation to the court. In this they were joined by the Christian congregations in Rome.

When the hour of the trial arrived, Paulus and Jason were escorted into the courtroom. Paulus was almost overcome with emotion at standing face to face with the ruler of the whole Roman world, but was able to bow respectfully before him and respond to his greeting. When called upon to testify, he reminded the Emperor that his defense was in writing and asked him as judge to follow his written copy, so there would be no misunderstanding of the case.

After hearing Paulus' entire defense, Caesar responded, "If this statement is true you should have been released at once. Why did you appeal to my court here in Rome?"

"The Jews tried to kill me in Jerusalem, but were prevented from accomplishing their purpose by soldiers from the Praetorium. Their purpose was to prevent a general riot. But when they learned that assassins were waiting in the streets to kill me, the commander sent me under escort to Caesarea. Both Felix and Festus were convinced of my innocence but did not release me in deference to the desire of the Jews. I was aware of the plots against me, so when the governor was about to release me, I appealed to you knowing I would be transported to Rome and protected until I appeared before you, O Noble Caesar."

"What will you do if I release you?"

"I will stay out of Judea. I doubt if they can do me any harm in the Roman Empire, since I am a Roman citizen."

After a long pause, the Emperor questioned Paulus again: "I have heard it said that this Jesus you worship claims to be a king and will set up a new government that will rule the whole world."

"Pilate accused Jesus of this, but he answered clearly: 'My kingdom is not of this world.' Jesus' kingdom is the kingdom of truth. It is a kingdom of the heart. Those who believe in Him will live an honest and true life in this world and then will go to live with him forever."

"Do you believe all of this?"

"Yes, Your Honor, I do with all my heart."

"What will you do if I release you?"

"I will spend the rest of my life preaching the Good News I have declared to you today. I am persuaded that what I have declared to you is the truth and that all who believe it will be better citizens and will help to make the Roman Empire a better place to live."

The Emperor sat for many minutes with a bowed head and knitted brow. At last he raised his eyes and stated firmly to the prisoner: "I cannot understand all you have said, but I believe you are sincere, and certainly innocent of all charges made against you. You are free to go, and may your God be with you."

Chapter VIII
Spain and Beyond

"Spain! Here we come!" shouted Jason as they entered Paulus' house.

"I am anxious to see Spain too," replied Paulus as he looked around the house that had become a comfortable home and office for him during his wait for the trial, "but we can't go quite yet. We have to dispose of all this and then go see Hannah as we promised."

"Oh, yes, of course, I am just so excited I can't think straight yet."

"Are you thinking of Spain, or are you dreaming of a pair of soft brown eyes?"

"Well, let's get busy. I think you are thinking of soft, brown eyes too," countered Jason as a pink glow crept over his cheeks.

"Luke, can you find a small house near one of our churches where we could store all these documents and personal possessions? On second thought it should be large enough to serve as headquarters for you and the rest of our company whenever they are in Rome."

"Start packing things up then. I already have an idea where to look. I'll be back as soon as I can," replied Luke.

Just then Lucius walked in and began to pound his friends on the back as he congratulated them on winning the trial. Paulus, ever practical, suddenly exclaimed: "Could you find passage for us on a fast ship for Tarsus? We promised to go see Hannah as soon as the trial was over."

"No sooner said than done," replied Lucius, as he again pounded Paulus on the back and headed out the door.

Now the two travelers began to sort out what they would need on the trip to Tarsus and then store the rest in boxes and trunks to be taken to the new location. "My, there is a lot of stuff to go through," complained Jason as they went through desks and store rooms. "We will have to get the rest of the men in here to sort out what belongs to each one of them."

"All we can do now is take care of our personal possessions. They will all have to sort out what they want to keep and pack it themselves," replied Paulus. "It's a good thing they are all here in Rome now."

"I've found it! I've found it!" shouted Luke as he rushed into the house later that day. "The church nearest the Catacombs has been looking for a larger place of worship. They have located a large warehouse. On the rear of the property there is a house that has been used for storage. That house is large enough to accommodate all of your extra clothing and property when you are not using it. It will also serve as an office for the pastor. The only problem is that the rent of the property is more than they can afford. Could you possibly help them with the rent?"

"I am sure we can. Jason, you know all about our income and expenses. Why don't you go with Luke and see what we can work out?"

That evening Lucius returned with the good news that he had secured their passage on a small ship that was leaving in two days for a direct sail to Tarsus. Now the packing began in earnest and the two travelers were soon on their way.

* * * * * *

The next day Jason remonstrated with his uncle: "You are going to wear out your sandals and be so tired and sleepy you won't be able to enjoy seeing Aunt Hannah if you don't stop pacing the deck and get some sleep."

"I know, but I just can't seem to be able to relax and sit down, let alone sleep."

"But you must. I'll get you a cup of hot tea, and we'll sit down here where you can feel the soft breezes and relax a bit."

To his surprise, Paulus found himself relaxing as they sat together in close companionship and soon began to fall asleep. Jason spread his coat in a sheltered spot on deck and succeeded in getting Paulus to lie down. He was soon rewarded by seeing that his uncle was fast asleep.

Two days later the ship pulled up to the docks in Tarsus. Paulus was the first person down the gang plank. Running up behind him, Jason shouted: "I'll take care of the baggage and will then go by the office to see how things are going while you get acquainted with Hannah again."

Paulus was so eager to get home that he started out on the run. He soon found, though, that during his two years of inactivity (since he was chained to the soldier who guarded him) had left him overweight and unable to run more than a few steps. He still walked on as fast as he could. When he reached the house he ran up the steps to the porch and burst through the door shouting: "Hannah, Hannah, I'm home. Where are you?"

Back in the kitchen Hannah was at first startled to hear a man burst into the house, calling her name, so grabbing up the heaviest ladle she could find, she started for the parlor. As she entered the room she saw a man rushing toward her with his arms open wide and a huge smile on his face. She knew him at once, and dropping the ladle, rushed into his arms whispering: "Oh Saul, I am so glad to see you."

"You are not any happier than I am. Sometimes I came to think I could not live another day without seeing you and feeling your love and support."

"Since you are here, the trial must now be over. Tell me how it went and what the final verdict was."

"Jason and I decided that it would be better to write out my defense, which we did. Then we made a copy for the emperor, one for me, and an extra copy in case it was needed. Caesar was impressed with the clarity of the case, and granted me a full pardon. I have brought a copy for you. On it I have also written out his verdict. Here it is for you to keep and study over at your leisure."

When Jason arrived at the house that evening, he found the excited couple still totally engrossed in animated conversation and expressions of love and devotion for each other.

"When are we going to eat? I am famished," called out Jason.

"Oh, dear," sighed Hannah. "I was just starting to fix something to eat this morning when I heard a wild man burst through the door. I grabbed up the biggest ladle I had and ran to confront him. When I recognized who it was I must have dropped the ladle. Sure enough, there it is on the floor yet. Give it to me Jason. Now let's all go to the kitchen and see what we can stir up."

Together they were able to put together a satisfactory meal and then continued their visit until dark, when they all realized it had been a long and exciting day and now they were all needing a good night's sleep.

It was several days before they were able to book passage on a ship headed back to Rome. Even then they were reluctant to leave, but once on their way they spent most of the time planning their trip to Spain and deciding on their activities once they were there.

Besides his desire to see Maria, Jason was anxious to tap the large market for tents with the Army in Gaul and Spain, and preach the Gospel of salvation in the synagogues in those areas.

* * * * * *

As soon as they arrived in Rome, Luke took them to their new house near the Catacombs. "This house is adequate for office and living quarters for those of us who will be in Rome from time to time, but it is too small to store all of our belongings," he explained. "Since is close to the Catacombs, we have decided to store some of our property there for now. Who knows if we will have to take refuge there ourselves before long.

"Everyone is expecting that Nero will be the next Emperor. If that happens we will all be in trouble. He is an angry, wicked man and has no respect for human life."

Because of this disquieting news, Jason, Paulus and their party rushed their preparations for the trip to Spain. They even decided to go by ship rather than take the long overland route through Gaul. Lucius was becoming well adapted to his task of taking new orders for tents, so he planned to make a special trip to Gaul once they were established in Spain.

* * * * * *

At last Paulus was actually on his way to Spain. He and his companions were enamored with the balmy breezes and luscious tropical foliage of the southern coastline of Spain [now known as the Spanish Riviera]. But they could not linger there as they were headed for the central highlands where Maria lived.

Paulus and his companions began at once to search out the synagogues in the area and begin their evangelistic activities. They were amazed at the number of Jews in Spain, and delighted to see that they responded readily to the preaching of Paulus and his helpers. Lucius also found a good response to his tents and soon had many orders to forward to Rome and Tarsus.

But the most excited of all was Jason, who found Maria at home. She welcomed him with open arms, and they were soon talking about building a future together. When Jason began to press for the setting of a wedding date, however, he was surprised at the reluctance on Maria's part to respond to his enthusiasm.

"But, I thought you were agreed that we should be married soon," expostulated Jason.

"Well, yes, I want to marry you, but I hesitate to rush into marriage until we have had time to decide where we will live, and whether you will be home or away on evangelistic trips most of the time."

So it was that Jason spent much time in prayer and in conversation with Maria and her father. Finally their conversations turned to the message Paulus was presenting in the synagogues of the area, and the many of both Jews and Greeks who were accepting Paulus' message and forming new Christian churches.

After several days of intense Bible study and prayer, both Maria and her father were persuaded that Jesus really was the Son of God and the Messiah of not only the Jews, but of people of all nations and languages.

One morning as Maria prayed and sought for guidance from the Scriptures, her eyes fell upon the story of Ruth, the Moabitess, who was talking with her mother-in-law, Naomi. Naomi had migrated to Moab with her family because of the famine in Israel. There her husband and both of her sons had died. Now she was on her way back to Israel and was bidding a reluctant goodbye to her two daughters-in-law. Orpah turned back sadly, but Ruth clung to Naomi and declared: "Thy people shall be my people, and thy God my God."[1]

As she thought and prayed about this verse, Maria was more and more impressed that God was calling her to do as Ruth did—leave her comfortable home and follow her husband—perhaps even to unknown lands and help him spread the exciting news of salvation to all, Gentiles as well as Jews.

Maria could hardly contain her enthusiasm as she ran to her father and tearfully explained to him the revelation that had come to her as she read the story of Ruth. Together they talked and prayed for God to guide them and for His will to be done. At last her father, placing his hand under her chin, and lifted her head until they were both gazing into each other's eyes.

"You really believe that God is calling you to do this, don't you Maria?"

"Yes, father, with all my heart."

"Then, let's go and find Jason, and see if he will agree to take you with him on his travels."

A few days later, Jason was surprised to see Maria and her father in the crowd he was addressing. Paulus had begun to give him the responsibility of presenting the message of salvation to the Gentiles and had been more and more impressed with the clarity and effectiveness of his message.

Maria and Maimonides remained a part of the large crowd assembled on the plain until the service was over. As soon as he finished ministering to those who remained to consult with the evangelists, Jason and Paulus hurried to where Maria and her father were waiting for them. Maria ran to Jason with outstretched arms while Paulus and her father greeted each other affectionately.

"Could we find a place where we could talk seriously without being disturbed?" inquired Maimonides.

"I'm sure we can," replied Paulus, as he led them to a tent they had prepared for rest during the meetings. "Lucius, could you stand guard before the tent to ask any callers to wait until our consultation is over?"

"Now, what is it that you have made this long trip about?" queried Paulus, "Not that we can't make a good guess," he continued as he looked at Jason and Maria who were gazing expectantly into each other's eyes.

"You all know that Jason and Maria have been in love for a long time, but Jason's traveling has seemed an impediment to their being together," replied Maimonides. "However, lately she has received what she believes is the answer to this problem. I'll let her explain it to you and then we can discuss it and pray about it."

"During my devotions a few days ago," began Maria, "I was reading the story of Naomi and Ruth the Moabitess. You all know that Naomi and her family had moved to Moab because of a famine in Israel. There they lived in comfort and their two sons married Moabites women. Then tragedy struck. Naomi's husband and both of her sons died, leaving her alone with two daughters in law. She decided to return home to Israel and dismissed her two daughters-in-law so they could go home and start their life over again. One of them did so at once, but the other one, Ruth, said to her mother in law, 'Entreat me not to leave thee, or to return from following thee: for whither thou goest, I will go: and whether thou lodgest, I will lodge: thy people shall be my people, and thy God my God.'"[2]

"It was the last phrase that impelled me to come to you, Jason. Thy people shall be my people, and thy God my God."

"But that wasn't the end of the story, Maria. Ruth followed Naomi to Israel, and found a husband," shouted Jason.

"Jason, that's what we are here to talk to you about," smiled Maria's father.

"But Maria has told me she is reluctant for us to marry, if I am going to insist on going on with these meetings, while she pines at home, and I can understand and sympathize with how she feels, yet I can't feel that I should abandon my calling—at least not at this time."

"But you don't understand," pleaded Maria. "I want to go with you. I feel sure that my testimony will help many decide to follow Jesus. I would like also to have an opportunity to present your message to the doubtful ones, especially the women and children."

"That sounds wonderful," Jason reasoned, "but I don't think you understand about the lack of home comforts, the irregular hours, the hunger and exhaustion, that we experience. There are days when we scarcely have time to eat or rest."

"That convinces me more than ever that you need a woman in the camp. I would make sure that you had time for regular meals (I would like to show you that I am a good cook) and rest at night, as well as participate in the presentation of the message and counsel with the women. Why don't Jason and I prepare something to eat now while you counsel with those who are waiting so patiently outside."

When they reached the supply tent Jason and Maria were dismayed to find only a few eggs, a slice or two of ham, some wilted onions and a few other dried up vegetables and seasonings. "Well, I believe I can make a stew and boil these eggs for tonight, but we will need a supply of food for tomorrow and the days ahead. Go call my father while I make out a list of the supplies we need. He is used to buying the food for our house at home. I will be making a list for him while you find him and bring him here."

Maimonides came as soon as he was called. "Do you have a pack mule or a cart to carry the produce," he inquired.

"No, we just fill a bag and sling it over our shoulders" replied Jason.

As soon as Maria finished the list she was making, her father took it and inquired about the way to the nearest town. As the others were finishing their evening meal, he arrived back in the camp. Everyone was surprised to see him driving a donkey hitched to a cart piled high with foodstuffs as well as some new pots and pans and an iron kettle for baking biscuits.

"What is all this for?" asked Paulus.

"You will need all this to have proper meals, and I will not leave until my daughter has what she needs to feed her husband and his friends," smiled Maimonadese.

"Do I understand you are giving your consent for your daughter to marry Jason at once and remain with our company?" asked Paulus.

"There doesn't seem to be any other option," smiled Maimonides.

"You are irresistible, my dear," murmured Jason.

"You are right, my son, she is irresistible," assented her father.

"But we don't have any wedding clothes here!"

"We'll wear just what we have on. We don't want to look like rich people before this crowd, do we? You surely have a clean outfit in your baggage. I can smooth it out tonight and also take the wrinkles out of my dress. I am sure there is enough flour in what papa brought today to make a huge batch of sugar buns tonight, so we can invite everyone here to the wedding and the celebration right after the service."

* * * * * *

Great excitement prevailed as everyone began to offer to do anything they could to further the plans for the wedding. Finally Lucius cleared his throat and remarked. "I have some news that is very serious and may make a difference in the plans we are all talking about, but I have withheld it until now because I couldn't bear to inject fear into this joyous occasion. As you all know, Nero has been made the new

Caesar in Rome. Everyone was concerned because he is a violent and angry man, but no one expected him to make such an extreme and dangerous decision. He has declared that he is God and must be obeyed and worshiped as such. Anyone who fails to do this is immediately put to death. He seems to be especially targeting Jews and Christians."

"Are they succumbing to such a vile threat?"

"Indeed they are not, but he is slaughtering them in droves. Some of them have managed to escape the city. Many others are taking refuge in the Catacombs."

"Do the soldiers go in after them?"

"Some of them did at first, but they now refuse to enter and search for them."

"Why?"

"None of the ones who went in ever came back out."

After a long and painful silence, Paulus announced quietly: "I must go back at once. They need me now more than ever."

"I will go with you," announced Jason.

"No, no, Jason. You promised never to leave me," Maria cried as she collapsed weeping in his arms.

"Maria is right, Jason. Besides I have been wanting to ask you to take over here in Spain so I could continue work elsewhere. I want to see what can be done in Crete. I am sure Lucius will act as guide to us since he will know how to contact the Christians in hiding. I will take Titus with us and perhaps Luke and some others." Then turning to Lucius he inquired, "Is Nero trying to put this new rule into effect anywhere outside of Rome?

"I think he plans to eventually, but I have not found anyone who knows about it outside of Rome, except in an army camp or two."

"Then we must work as fast as we can before this evil spreads further. I will not leave though before the wedding nor until Jason and Maria are installed officially as the leaders of our cause in Spain."

With everyone working the rest of the day and most of the night, everything was in readiness by the time the crowd began to assemble the following day. Paulus sat back on the sidelines as Jason and Maria took charge of the proceedings. Their testimonies and messages were greeted enthusiastically by the large crowd and many were those who accepted the good news of salvation.

At the close of the meeting, Paulus stepped forward and announced that Jason and Maria were to be married and that they all were invited to participate in the wedding festivities. A great shout went up as the crowd received this momentous news, and it took a while to quiet them down enough to proceed with the wedding ceremony.

The new couple waited patiently to receive the congratulations of each member of the congregation and express their happiness for the opportunity of being their new pastors. At last they were escorted to the new tent that had been prepared for them where they collapsed into each other's arms as they wept and laughed together.

While Paulus was eager to return to Rome to shepherd the believers there, he was also anxious to see Jason and Maria well-established to care for the churches in Spain. He was greatly encouraged when Maimonides announced his decision to join his daughter and Jason. His experience and good standing with the people and the governing bodies of Spain would be an asset to the new churches and help protect them from the furies of Nero.[3]

Chapter IX
Final Imprisonment

While Paulus was anxious to get to Rome to comfort and protect the Christians there, he was wise enough to allow Lucius to plan their trip and take the leadership of their party. They decided to take Titus and Timothy with them. There were others who wanted to join them, but Lucius decided that they would be able to travel more safely with a small party.

"Traveling overland is long and arduous," Lucius admitted, as he laid out his plan. "But it will be safer than traveling by ship and being inspected at each port of call. I have secured a cart to haul some tents. These will furnish us with shelter at night and give us samples to use for taking orders in army camps along the way. If we do some business, it will make our journey appear to be merely a sales venture."

Since Paulus was anxious about the new church in Ephesus, they decided to visit it before proceeding to Rome. They found a large and flourishing congregation there but soon noticed that it lacked a good leader. After consulting with his companions and the church leaders, Paulus decided to leave Timothy to organize the church and the new ones springing up in Asia Minor.

When this was decided, a general assemble of the church was called. Paulus addressed the large crowd and then introduced Timothy to them and commissioned him as the bishop of Ephesus.

With the Ephesian church in good hands, the small group continued on their journey. Finally, they arrived in the outlying districts of Rome. Lucius showed the party how to skirt the city and approach the Catacombs by little-known trails. At last he found a place where they could conceal their cart and horses. Leaving the rest of the party with them, Lucius stole softly to a little-known opening he knew of. As he expected, it was guarded by alert sentries, but he was able to identify himself and was allowed to enter. Finding a good-sized colony of Christians comfortably hidden there, he returned at once to bring Paulus, Timothy, and Titus inside to meet the eager Christians.

To their delight, they found that Peter, the Big Fisherman, was there and was recognized as the leader of the group. They also learned that most of the Christians had fled Rome and gone to live in the countryside or even to other countries where the ban on Jews and Christians was not yet in effect.

Satisfied that the Church in Rome was safely settled in the Catacombs, Paulus and his party slipped away during the night and worked their way without difficulty to the lovely island of Crete. Here they found that travelers from Rome had already been preaching the Gospel to Jews and Greeks alike. They added their help and experience to the rapid expansion of the Church and to organizing each group with leaders and workers from within the group.

Paulus was especially gratified to see how well Titus assisted in these activities and was soon putting him forward as the leader and organizer of the new churches. Soon he felt confident that he could leave Titus to continue the good work in Crete[1] while he visited other countries around the Mediterranean Sea.

They were moderately successful in spreading the gospel in countries both on the northern and southern rim of the Mediterranean. However it soon became evident that Nero was trying to put the new ban on Jews and Christians, not only in Rome, but in all countries under Roman jurisdiction. Two or three times Paulus' band narrowly escaped arrest by suspicious officials. After much prayer, Paulus felt that he needed to return to Rome and join the Christians established in the Catacombs. He released Lucius, who had been wanting to tour Gaul and establish a center there for making and selling army tents.

* * * * * *

Not a twig snapped as Paulus stealthily approached the secret entrance to the catacombs. But as he parted the bushes in front of the entrance, he came face-to-face with a Roman sentry. Immediately, he was surrounded and bound.

"I am a Roman citizen," Paulus protested, hoping to be released.

"What is your name?" a soldier asked.

"Paulus, I am a tentmaker."

"Paulus! The Emperor will be particularly glad to hear of your arrest. We will take you to him at once."

* * * * * *

In a deep pit in the worst prison in Rome, Paulus languished while Nero considered how to destroy him. After several months, knowing he would never be released to travel again, Paulus wrote out a document to send to Titus officially appointing him the head of the church in Crete.[2] He also wrote to Jason, commending him for the good work he, and his family, were carrying on in Spain. Enclosed with it was a document recommending that he be accepted as "Jason of Tarsus, Apostle to Spain."[3]

His last official act was to write a letter to Timothy in which he tacitly admitted that there is no hope this time of an acquittal from Caesar's decree of death to Christians who would not recognize him as God. It was this letter which closes with the apostle's valedictory:

I am now ready to be offered,
And the time of my departure is at hand.
I have fought a good fight,
I have finished my course,
I have kept the faith.

Henceforth there is laid up for me
A crown of righteousness,
Which the Lord will give me in that day:
And not to me only
But unto all them also that love his appearing.[4]

Chapter X
Jason—Apostle to Spain

After completing his missives to Titus, Jason, and Timothy, Paulus poured out his heart in a final, loving letter to his wife Hannah. Then he called for Lucius and another nephew, Sosipater.[1]

"My dear friends," he cried as he saw them. "Thank God; He has made it possible for you to come. I was afraid you would be arrested when you asked to see me and have been praying fervently for your safety. How is the Church bearing up under this severe persecution?"

"Many have been arrested and are to be sacrificed in the arena. But many others have been hiding in the catacombs and others have left Rome and are melting into the countryside, taking the message of their faith with them," answered Lucius.

"Here is a final message to my wife and letters for Titus in Crete, for Timothy in Ephesus, and Jason in Spain," explained Paulus. "Can I count on you to deliver them? I have prayed for you earnestly and am sure Jesus will be with you and protect you."

Both Sosipater and Lucius embraced Paulus fervently and then left on their mission, grieving that they would see their friend and mentor no more on this earth.

* * * * * *

As soon as they were able to escape Rome without detection, the two emissaries breathed sighs of relief and began their search for a ship sailing for the island of Crete. This proved to be easily done and they were soon on their way.

* * * * * *

"Titus, Titus," shouted Lucius as they approached the building where the Church in Crete met for worship. "It's so good to see you. Uncle Paulus said that you would probably be back from your trip to Dalmatia.[2] We were hoping to deliver this document from him to you in person. . . .You seem to be meeting for worship. Hasn't the news of Caesar's orders reached here yet?"

"What order?" queried Titus, as he noted the anxious expression on the faces of his friends.

"Caesar has declared himself to be a god, and no one is allowed to worship any other god. As you will surely understand, thousands of Christians in Rome have refused to do so. They have been arrested and will soon be executed. The rest have hidden in the catacombs or fled to the countryside."

"Where is Paulus?"

"He is still under arrest and is now convinced that there is no hope of his release. He has sent us here with a letter documenting his appointment of you. Here it is," Sosipater announced as he handed over the sealed package.

With trembling hands, Titus opened the package and read the startling words of the great Apostle to the Gentiles.

"But what does this mean?" he cried.

"As you saw, it was sealed," replied Lucius. "I know it is an appointment for you, but I know no more than that. Please read it aloud so we will know what it says."

After perusing the document carefully, Titus burst into tears and handed the document to Lucius, saying brokenly, "Here, you read it and tell me what it means."

After reading the document carefully, Lucius placed his hand kindly on Titus' shoulder and said softly, "My dear friend, the great Apostle Paulus, realizing he will soon be executed, has given you his authority over the churches in Crete and prays God to be with you in this great task. We both wish to congratulate you and are happy you have been chosen for this task. Let us inform them of you appointment."

"Let's wait until tomorrow so I can form some sort of address to the assembly."

* * * * * *

Titus and the messengers from Rome announced a special assembly of the church for the following day and then retired into seclusion for prayer and consultation. When the appointed time arrive, Lucius and Sosipater first explained the new government regulation declaring Nero to be God and requiring all peoples to worship him only. Refusal to do so would mean certain death. They also informed them, with great sadness, that hundreds of Christian in Rome had no doubt already been thrown to the lions in the Coliseum and that their beloved Paulus was confined in the Mamertime Prison or possibly already executed.

* * * * * *

It was late that evening before Lucius and Sosipater could quiet the crowd enough to be able to present Titus to them with these words: "Dear friends and fellow Christians. We have more news for you, and this is glorious news. Paulus has sent us to inform you that, since he is no longer able to be your leader, he is appointing some of his competent associates as overseers of the Church in their area. You will be glad to hear that he has appointed your beloved Titus as the bishop of the churches in Crete. It gives me great pleasure to introduce to you all Titus, Bishop of Crete."

When the crowd had quieted enough so Titus could address them, he pledged his love to them and accepted the great honor and responsibility placed upon him.

The inspiring and emotional visit to Crete was repeated in Ephesus as Timothy read the beloved apostle's last letter to him and the visitors comforted and exhorted the people to continue strong in the gospel, as Paul had always encouraged them to do. As Lucius and Sosipater left Epehsus, Timothy was setting people in charge of the flock so that he could go immediately to Paulus, as he had requested in his letter.[3]

* * * * * *

Lucius and Sosipater were anxious to be on their way to Spain but had one more important message to deliver—to Paulus' wife, Hannah—before beginning the long and dangerous trip to Spain.

Since Lucius carried orders for tents from army camps around Rome, they now traveled as tentmakers and had no trouble booking passage to Tarsus, the headquarters of the profitable business.

Their first call in Tarsus was to the house of Hannah.

"Lucius, Lucius," she cried as she rushed to his side with open arms. "Where is my dear husband, Saul?"

"I am deeply sorry to have to tell you that he has been arrested again and is now being held in the terrible Mamertime Prison."

"Then I will go to him at once," declared Hannah.

"Oh no," both Lucius and Sosipater exclaimed, "You would no doubt be arrested and thrown to the lions in the arena."

"But why? I am a Roman citizen. Surely they would let me see my husband."

"They would ask you if you were a Christian. And, if so, you would be ordered to worship Nero."

"Worship Nero? Not on your life. I worship God."

"That is just the trouble. Nero has proclaimed that he is God and that everyone—especially Jews and Christians—must worship him only. If any refuse, they are thrown to the lions. Hundreds have been killed already. I am sorry to say it, but your husband may have already been executed. Your only safety is to continue with your tent making and to meet with your fellow Christians only in secret."

"Could you arrange for the leaders of your churches to meet with us, so we can inform them of this danger and plan how to avoid arrest?" asked Lucius.

* * * * * *

For several anxious days they met secretly with Christians in and around Tarsus. Then, with their mission in this city completed, and having received a sum of money from the family to deliver to Jason, they were free to head for Spain. Fortunately, they were carrying tents for various army units in Asia Minor, so they could pass as businessmen.

"I think it would be better is we sailed to Ephesus and then follow the Roman road to the army camps in the interior, even if it means back-tracking quite a ways. I have visited the Christian churches between Tarsus and Ephesus more than once and might be recognized if we traveled overland to Ephesus. We will have to limit ourselves to delivering these tents to the army camps this time."

* * * * * *

After landing at Ephesus, the two travelers cautiously worked their way through Macedonia and Greece, taking orders and delivering tents. They noticed that the nearer they approached Rome the more they heard of Christians being arrested.

"This persecution of Christians and Jews seems to be spreading first though Rome and then through the countryside," remarked Lucius. "We are going to have to find a ship that sails west without stopping in Rome."

* * * * * *

After many days and much discouragement, Sosipater finally found a ship in Corinth preparing to sail to southern

Spain. Bursting into their camp, he shouted, "God has answered our prayers. I have found a ship sailing for Spain."

Grateful for their good fortune, Lucius and Sosipater boarded the ship with light hearts. "The captain tells me he is not stopping at the regular ports of Spain but has a special cargo for a small port on the extreme southern shore of Spain," announced Lucius after they had been sailing for several days.

"How are we going to find Jason and the Christians?" worried Sosipater as the ship approached the small port and prepared to dock.

"Well, I remember that the region where Maimonides lives is known as La Mancha and it is in the central part of Spain," responded Lucius, "so we will need to head north."

As they traveled day after day they noticed that there were very few army camps in this sparsely settled area, nor any well-traveled roads. Each night they prayed fervently for guidance but the only answer they could get was to proceed farther north.

When they halted at noon one day after weeks of slow travel, Lucius declared, "It seems to me that the countryside around here looks vaguely familiar. Have you noticed the mountains off to our left? They look like the ones near Maimonides' ranch."

"Really?" exclaimed Sosipater. "Let's bear a little to the left and hurry on. Perhaps we are near where the Christians are camped."

Soon Lucius recognized the entrance to the valley where the Christians were camped when Jason and Maria were married. To their surprise they were halted by an armed guard who shouted, "Halt! Who goes there?"

Started by the abrupt challenge and fearing they had stumbled onto an army camp, Lucius at once began to display their sample tents and requested to speak with their commanding officer.

The guard, who had been observing the travelers carefully, suddenly broke into a hearty laugh and shouted, "Lucius! We have been wondering when you would return. We were afraid you must have been captured because of Nero's new orders."

"Are they now being enforced here?"

"One of our herders, who had joined the Roman army before we learned of Jesus' death and resurrection, was mustered out of the army about a year ago. He came home and, when he found us worshiping Christ, he told us a frightful story of what had occurred in his camp. Come on down to the camp. He will tell you the story."

Many joyful embraces later, the newly-arrived travelers were able to turn their attention to the narrative of Joshua, the former soldier.

"We were camped in Southern Gaul on the shore of a large lake. It was winter; snow covered the ground and the lake was frozen over solidly. During this time, inspectors arrived from Rome. They informed our captain that the new emperor, Nero, had declared himself to be God and that everyone must worship him. Any who refused were to be immediately executed.

"Everything went well until a troop of Christian soldiers were called. These troops belonged to a specialized force that was often called upon to take part in dangerous and fearful combat with the barbarian forces in the area. Twenty one of these soldiers were the most sincere and effective of the members of the battalion. As the captain expected, they without hesitation refused to salute Nero as God, explaining that they served the God of the whole universe.

"The inspector demanded that they be immediately executed. The captain tried every argument he could think of to get the inspector to change his mind, but to no avail. Finally the inspector shouted: 'It doesn't matter how you do it but you must execute them at once.'

"As he tried to find a humane way to carry out the sentence, a strange revelation seemed to come to him. He called the men together and explained to them the verdict of the inspector. Then he said he was forced to condemn them to death, so he ordered them to disrobe and march out onto the frozen lake. They were to stay there until they all died, which he hoped would not be long due to the severely cold wind that was blowing and the frozen surface of the lake.

"They quietly disrobed, but as they started marching out onto the lake, they began to sing:

'Twenty-one soldiers of Christ are we,
To live for Him or to die for Him.
Twenty-one soldiers of Christ are we,
To live for Him or to die for Him.'

"Soon they were out of sight due to the blowing snow and the dense haze that had settled over the lake. Before long, the soldiers on the shore descried a naked figure emerging from the fog. 'Give me my clothes! Lead me to the fire!' he cried. 'I can't stand it any longer.'

The angry soldiers began to express their surprise and shock at the weakness of the renegade Christian and no one lifted a hand to help him. They became silent as they heard the song from the lake change to:

'Twenty soldiers of Christ are we
To live for Him or to die for Him.'

"Then to their amazement and surprise they saw their captain suddenly begin to tear his own clothes from his body. Lifting his voice, he began to sing as he marched out on the frozen lake:

'TWENTY-ONE soldiers of Christ are we
To live for Him or to die for Him.' "[4]

There was silence for a moment. Then Lucius spoke: "It's good that you are aware that persecution has begun in this land," said Lucius. "My own feelings are that you will probably not be molested unless you call attention to your activities or flout your opposition to Nero. I am sure you are already aware of this and are doing what you can to spread the Good News of the Gospel without being confrontational with unbelievers or challenging the authorities."

"We have already been taking some precautions," explained Maimonides. "I have left my estate in the hands of caretakers. My stock have been sequestered in hidden valleys except for a few we keep with us for food and milk. Our meetings are held in out-of-the-way places. It is a wonder to all of us how the people get word of the meetings and come to them, seemingly without fear, but we will be even more careful in the future."

"I know you will. Now I would like to tell you the real reason for our coming at this time. Paulus now realizes that his career of spreading the Gospel to the world has come to the end. He knows that there is no chance that he will be released from prison this time. His execution will be soon if it has not already occurred. But he wanted to commend his mission to trusted men and women who will carry it on even after his death. I have already delivered a missive from Paulus to Titus in Crete, naming him the superintendent of the work in that country. We also delivered a letter to Timothy, confirming his appointment as pastor in Ephesus. He is probably with Paulus as we speak, since Paulus asked him to come.

"Now I have come here with sealed orders for you, Jason. Here are your orders. Please read them and inform us all of their contents so we can help you in any way we can."

With these gracious words, Lucius handed over to Jason a sealed package that Paulus had entrusted him to deliver.

Jason stood quietly for a few long moments, trying to quiet his beating heart and dry his weeping eyes. Finally he conquered his emotions to the extent that he could break the seal on the package and read Paul's recognition of him as Jason of Tarsus, Apostle to Spain.[5]

He stared in awe and gratitude at the confirmation of the call that he had carried in his heart. He handed the document to Maria with shaking hands as he fell to his knees in tears, thanking the Lord for the honor and earnestly requesting his grace to carry this responsibility.

Maria read the commission aloud to the others then dropped to her knees beside her husband with words of encouragement and support. Her father also knelt beside him. Reminding him of God's promises, they also assured him of their loyalty and support.

In the succeeding days a small group of leaders of the Church were called together to discuss the future of their lives and mission in the face of the dangers presented by Nero's savage policy. Because of their love for Spain and the compulsion to share Christ there, Jason and Maria were reluctant to consider leaving. However, after some days of fasting and prayer, they felt led to take refuge elsewhere for a period of time. The group decided to send scouts in search of such a new homeland.

The scouting party trudged northward into sparsely settled territory until they finally came to the high range of mountains that separated Spain from the rest of Europe. As they penetrated the rugged mountains they discovered rich, hidden valleys that promised safe retreats from invading armies because the mountain passes were narrow and rugged and easily defended. Hurrying home they recommended these mountain valleys as a safe retreat from the armies of Rome.

Jason was delighted with the prospects described by the scouts, so he called a mass meeting of the Church and its leaders to discuss this option. Most of the people were glad for this opportunity to evade the distress caused by Nero's policies. So plans were set in motion to settle in the Apennine mountain valleys. A few timid souls decided to stay at home rather than make such a drastic move, but soon the Church was on the move.

* * * * * *

While this migration was going on, Lucius and Sosipater hurried back to Tarsus to inform the family of Jason and Maria's new location and of the plan suggested by Maimonides for sending funds to them there.

Upon arrival, they greeted a shaken Hannah. "Aunt Hannah! What is wrong? Have you received word about Uncle Saul?"

"Yes!" she reported. "Timothy made the journey here from Rome to personally break the news to me that my beloved Saul has been . . . He has been . . . beheaded."

For the next several days, Paulus' wife and his two friends consoled one another, and Hannah shared with them all that Timothy had told her about Paul's last days. Then Lucius and Sosipater journeyed together back to Spain. It took them several days to locate Jason and the Christians who were making their way slowly to the mountains.

Lucius gave the stricken Christians a detailed account of Paulus' last days and explained that since he was a Roman citizen they could not crucify him so he was beheaded instead. Peter, however, who had also been apprehended, was condemned to be crucified. This aged apostle, however, refused to be crucified in the usual way, insisting he was not worthy to die like his Lord had on Calvary. Instead he insisted on being crucified with his head down.

After arranging with Maimonides for the transfer of funds, Lucius and Sosipater returned to Italy and to Tarsus. Jason and Maria and her father continued their trek to the mountains where they lived until the horrors of Nero's reign ended with his death. Then they gratefully returned to their former homes where they continued the Christianizing of Spain.

EPILOGUE

It will surely be of interest for readers in the Western Hemisphere to learn that the events referred to in this story, coupled with other important developments in the growth and influence of the Spanish nation, had an important influence on the discovery and civilization of the Americas.

The first major event, or series of events, that had a lasting effect on the nation of Spain came with the invasion of Attila the Hun and other of the barbarian tribes into what is now central Europe. These Gothic tribes not only overran northern Italy and destroyed the old Roman Empire, but also occupied Central and Western Europe in the 4th and 5th centuries. One division of these "barbarians" destroyed Rome and effectively put an end to the Roman Empire. When this occurred, the only entity left in Rome with any power at all was the Bishop of Rome (the Pope). He immediately used his authority as pope of the Christian Church to confront the invaders, and bring some semblance of stable authority to the city.

This stabilizing influence was soon expanded to include the rest of Europe, which was possible because most of these countries were already known as Christian nations. The situation was somewhat different in Spain however, since Spain was a peninsula divided from the rest of Europe by the Apennine Mountains and jutting southward until it practically closed the Mediterranean Sea from the Atlantic Ocean by the fortress of Gibraltar. Their relatively isolated position made them less vulnerable to the barbarian hoards that overran Central Europe.

At last one of the Gothic tribes found its way over the Apennine Mountains and took over the country of Spain. It is remarkable however that the Spaniards were able to absorb these invaders and for the most part Christianize them. It was a different story, however, when, some years later, the Mohammedans began to infiltrate the south of Spain across the narrow Straits of Gibraltar. First they established themselves on the Spanish Riviera, and then mounted a steady campaign to take over the rest of Spain. All the natives of Spain could do was to flee north and take refuge in the Apennine Mountains.

Finally, after the year 1000, the embattled Spaniards began to descend from their mountain hideouts and carve out for themselves small portions of northern Spain. They continued this until the time when King Ferdinand of the province of Castile married Queen Isabel of Aragon. By uniting their kingdoms and enlisting help from the other Northern provinces, they were finally able to drive the Moors out of Spain. For this, the Pope gave them the title of His Catholic Majesties. He also gave them many special favors, like the collection of the tithes (which was done by Roman authorities in other countries) and the appointment of bishops within their realm.

At about this time scientists became convinced that this planet we live on is round rather than flat. Most people rejected this as wild speculation, but a few began to believe it. One sailor (Christopher Columbus) decided to put it to the test by leading a fleet of ships to the west until they found the Indies. He tried to find sponsors for this venture in Italy, but was unable to inspire anyone to believe him. Finally he was able to convince Queen Isabella of Spain. She was so convinced that she is said to have sold many of her crown jewels to raise the funds necessary to purchase three ships (the Nina, the Pinta and the Santa Maria) and outfit them with men and supplies to sail to the Indies under the command of Christopher Columbus.

When Columbus happened upon a group of islands at the mouth of the Gulf of Mexico he thought he had reached the Indies, so called the inhabitants he found there "Indians." Later, when he realized his mistake he revised the name of the islands to "West Indies," but the name of the inhabitants is still used today.

Columbus and the Spanish explorers who followed him into Central and South America were ardent Roman Catholic Christians. The first thing they did upon discovering a new country was to declare it a Christian nation and teach the inhabitants to worship the crucifix and Holy Mary. Even today most of the countries of Central and South America have adopted their version of the Virgin Mary as the patron of their countries. For example, the patron of Mexico is the Virgin of Guadalupe, and that of the Dominican Republic is the Virgin of Altagracia.

This is not true, however of North America which was colonized by England and other central and northern European countries that represented Protestant Christianity.

Appendix I
Was the Apostle Paul Married?

This may seem to be a strange question to the majority of Bible readers today who are accustomed to the prevalent theory that Paul was not married and even that he recommended this state to the readers of his epistles. It also is used by the Roman Catholic Church to justify their ruling that their clerics must remain unmarried.

It is important to note, however, that Paul nowhere in his writings directly states that he is not married. There is only one reference in the Bible to Saul's wife and that one is usually interpreted today to mean that he was not a married man. This reference (in 1 Corinthians, Chapter 9) occurs during a discussion of marriage in response to a question from the Corinthian Church. In this case Saul makes it clear that his answer takes into account the profoundly licentious conduct of the citizens of Corinth at that time. Corinth was a port city where sailors disembarked after long voyages during which they had been denied all contact with women. Their sexual cravings were welcomed by innumerable temple prostitutes who offered their favors at the temple sites. This was considered an act of worship and their fees became a lucrative source of income for the temples they represented.

In this exceedingly immoral society, Saul states firmly that it is better for young virgins to remain unmarried so they could dedicate themselves to Christian service and thus assist in changing the immoral degeneracy in Corinth. So when Saul recommends that they "remain as I am" he does not mean they should not be married, but whether married or unmarried they should be, as he was, deeply dedicated to the service of Christ.

That this recommendation was meant for a specific church at a specific time is easily seen if we look at Paul's statements on marriage in other of his epistles. He says, for example, "Now the overseer [bishop] must be above reproach, the husband of but one wife. . . . He must manage his own family well and see that his children obey him with proper respect" (1 Tim. 3:1-4). (See also Colossians 3:18-21.)

Even more specific is the statement of Eusebius, who wrote the first book on ecclesiastical history about the time of Constantine. This book has long been considered the first and best book of the history of the Early Church.

In the above cited History, Eusebius states on page 115, "Clement indeed, [Clement of Alexandria] whose words we have just cited, after the above mentioned facts, next gives a statement of those apostles that continued in the marriage state, on account of those who set marriage aside. 'And will they,' says he, 'reject even the Apostles! Peter and Philip, indeed, had children. Philip also gave his daughters in marriage to husbands, and Paul does not demur in a certain epistle to mention his own wife, whom he did not take with him, in order to expedite his ministry the better.'"[1]

So it seems clear, from the above quotations, that the early church understood that Paul was indeed a married man, but that he had reasons to not take his wife with him in his travels. For example, he was probably unwilling to submit his wife to the privations—beatings, stonings, shipwrecks, etc. that he faced. It may also be that she continued his operations with the tent-making company, but refused, until after his arrest in Jerusalem, to allow any of his assets to be sent to her husband who, in the eyes of his family, had repudiated his Jewish faith.

Appendix II
Saul the Roman Citizen

We have already mentioned the fact that the Jewish inhabitants of Tarsus were all Roman citizens. This came about because of the policy of the Roman government to establish cities which would be centers of Roman influence in the Greek world. These cities, like Alexandria (in Egypt) and Antioch (in Syria), were to be models of Roman citizenship and influence.

Tarsus was chosen to be one of these cities because of its strategic location on the "silk road" from China to Europe. By routing these expensive fabrics, perfumes etc. down the Cilician Gates formed by the Cydnus river as it descended from the Taurus mountains to the sea, they were able to avoid the long and brigand-infested route through Asia Minor to Greece. From Tarsus this merchandise could be easily shipped by sea to Greece and Rome.

It had been decided that there needed to be a strong majority of competent business men and artisans to make these cities strong Roman cities. They would also need to be populated with people who were Roman citizens. It mattered not of what ethnic or religious background they were, they would all be granted full Roman citizenship.

So it was that the family of Saul of Tarsus and his relatives, who were Jewish citizens, were also given Roman citizenship. This made a great difference between Saul and his family and other Jews living outside Palestine who were not Roman citizens. It also led members of Saul's family to not just attend the Synagogue schools, but also the Greek university that operated in Tarsus. This was a great advantage for Saul and one of the reason God called him to be the apostle to the Gentiles.

It made it possible for him to travel anywhere in the Near East and the European lands that circled the Mediterranean without the need of a passport since they were all part of the Roman Empire. It guaranteed him access to the Roman court system and freedom from death by crucifixion. He was also given a Roman name, Paulus (Paul) that would identify him at once as a Roman citizen. He would thus avoid interrogation at border crossings as all the territory he traveled in his missionary endeavors belonged to the Roman Empire.

Appendix III
Saul the Pharisee

We know that the members of Saul's family were devout Jews. As such they would have been faithful attendees of the synagogue services and their son Saul would have gone to the synagogue school. At the age of 12 he would have become an adult in the eyes of the Law and would have begun to take part as a leader of the synagogue service. It is important to realize however that the term *adult* and the term *man* were very different in Hebrew families. An adult could lead in the Synagogue service, but he was not a man until he became 30 years old and was married.

This all seems strange to us, but becomes more understandable when we realize that we Americans have a similar system. Our young men do not reach full manhood and independence until they are 21 years old, but they are allowed certain privileges of manhood as early as 16 and 18—the right to drive a car, enlist in the armed forces or hold a job, for example.

The life of Saul becomes clearer when we realize this. Our first glimpse of him in the Scriptures calls him a young *man*.

The priests and Levites who were stoning Stephen entrusted their robes to the young man Saul while they threw stones at Stephen. I had always considered Saul at this time to be at most a young teen-ager. But he was already a young *man*. So he would have to have been at least 30 years old.

With this in mind we have to ask ourselves: "When did he leave Tarsus and go to Jerusalem, and why? It seems logical to conclude that he had already completed his religious (as well as his Greek studies) in Tarsus and had gone to Jerusalem to pursue his religious studies. Being now a man he was probably also married, but had left his wife in Tarsus while he did his graduate studies in religion in Jerusalem—at the feet of the greatest of all Jewish rabbis at the time—Gamaliel.

It would seem to me that it was here that he fully comprehended the difference between the Sadducees and the Pharisees. Among other things, the most glaring difference in Saul's mind was that the Pharisees believed in the doctrine of the resurrection, while the Sadducees did not.

It was Saul's conviction that the Pharisees were right on this point of law that made him the great preacher of the resurrection and the future life with the resurrected Christ, which he preached as the great apostle of the Gentiles. It is revealing to realize that Paul never preached about the Virgin Birth or the miraculous ministry of Christ while he was here on earth. Saul always preached about the glorified Christ and our privilege of also being glorified and living with him in his home in Heaven.

Appendix IV
Saul—A Member of the Sanhedrin

The Sanhedrin was in actuality the congress of the Jewish nation, but it was limited to the religious life of the people, since they were subject to the Roman government during Saul's time for all civil matters.

It was composed of 70 men, plus the reigning High Priest. During New Testament times there were four eligible high priests—Annas, Caiphas, John and Alexander. Which one of these was the reigning high priest was subject to the will of the Roman governor. Since the government had had trouble with the cooperation of Annas, he had been deposed and Caiphas installed in his place. When Paulus was called before the Sanhedrin later in his ministry, he had been away from Jerusalem for years and therefore did not know which of the eligible members of Annas' family was the current high priest. So his response to the high priest who was presiding was understandable—"I didn't know you were the high priest."

Another element of diversity that gave something of a democratic mixture of members in the Sanhedrin was the existence of political/religious parties—the Sadducees, the Pharisees and the Essenes. These had been political parties during the independence of the Jewish nation in the time of the Hasmonean dynasty (in the Intertestament period).

The Sadducees won the political battle and took on political power (which they were able to continue during the Roman period). The Pharisees then became a religious party and ruled the religious life of the people with their many interpretations of the Torah. The one cardinal doctrine of the Pharisees, that attracted Saul strongly, was their belief in the resurrection. We are indebted to this factor in Saul's religious training that made him willing to accept the appearance of the Resurrected Christ to him on the road to Damascus.

With this understanding of Paul's religious views we need to ask ourselves again: "Was Saul a member of the Sanhedrin?"

Our first view of Saul in the Bible was at the stoning of Stephen. It is unlikely that the priests who were stoning Stephen would have entrusted their robes to an unknown young man. It is probable that even at this time he had become a "young" member of the Sanhedrin. This seems to be brought out in Acts 8:1: "And Saul was giving approval to his [Stephen's] death." Saul was actually voting for Stephen's death by stoning!

Saul's membership in the Sanhedrin would also give authority and sanction to his ferreting out Christians in Jerusalem for execution and official papers authorizing him to expand his destructive activities to the city of Damascus.

APPENDIX V
DIANA OF THE EPHESIANS

Diana was the Roman name of the goddess of fertility whose statue is always shown with nipples covering all the front of her body to denote abundant fertility—not just among human beings, but also among plants and animals. Diana is the Roman name of the goddess known to the Greeks as Artemis and to the Egyptians as Isis.[1]

The temple of the goddess Diana in Ephesus was one of the wonders of the ancient world, said to have been 400 feet long and 200 feet wide. It was completely surrounded by Ionic pillars 60 feet high.[2]

It was silver miniatures of this statute that Demetrius and his silversmiths were selling to the crowds which came to worship before this famous shrine that lost their popularity when Paulus came preaching the Gospel of salvation through Christ. Seeing their livelihood disappearing spurred Demetrius and his followers to start a riot to try to expel Paulus and his followers from Ephesus.[3]

A recent (2008) visitor to the ruins of Ephesus—Mike Kubat, a deacon of Neighbors to Nations Community Church in Lincoln, Illinois—brought back a tradition he heard while visiting there. According to this tradition, Constantine, while building the Hagia Sofia in Constantinople which was to become the "Rome" of the Eastern Orthodox Church, transported a number of the beautiful pillars from the ruins of Diana's temple to Constantinople to use in the construction of this beautiful Christian Church.

The only trace that Mike found that might have been from the ruins of Ephesus or the temple of Diana was a simple block of mosaic that could have been a floor tile from some building on the ruins of this historic site.

Appendix VI
Maimonides

When I first began to study the influence of the Jewish faith, and later Christianity, on the nation of Spain, I was surprised to learn that even in the time of Jonah there apparently was a Jewish presence in the southern part of Spain.

Long before this delightful coast of southern Spain became known as the Spanish Riviera, there was a prosperous port, known as Tarshish in that region. When Jonah decided to flee from the presence of the Lord, he went down to the port of Joppa. There he found a ship already loading for a trip to Tarshish.

Many scholars believe that this settlement was on the balmy southern coast of Spain. It was considered at that time to be at the western edge of the world. But already a regular shipping lane had been establish from Joppa to Tarshish and Jonah had no trouble booking passage on a ship already loading for its voyage to that settlement.

I was also to find that the Jewish population soon spread to other parts of Spain. These devout Jews (and later Christians) were a settling influence on the religious and cultural development of Spain. In fact one of the families, who surname was Maimon, became a wealthy and stabilizing influence on medieval Spain. The famous member of this family, known as Moses Maimonides, was a doctor, rabbi, religious scholar, mathematician, astronomer, and commentator on the art of medicine.[1] He is regarded as one of the foremost rabbinical philosophers in Jewish history.[2] Even today, several hospitals in major cities in the United States and Canada bear his name.[3]

I have decided to use this name for the father of Jason's wife. I do not intend to imply that Jason's father-in-law was the famous Maimonides of Spanish history. I only decided to use his name to indicate that this fictional personality had influence in Spain similar to that of his famous namesake—an influence which benefited the infant Christian Church in that country.

APPENDIX VII
APOSTLES

What is an apostle? Who are they? Who appoints, equips, and sends them out?

Most of us, like myself, I believe, have thought that Jesus chose twelve men whom he selected to train while He was here on earth and to whom he could entrust his mission when he ascended back into Heaven. They were further equipped on the day of Pentecost when they were filled with the Holy Spirit.

So we felt that Paul was assuming too much when he proclaimed himself the "apostle" to the Gentiles. Well, perhaps we could accept his claim, since he really did see Jesus on the road to Damascus and was given a commission to evangelize the Gentiles. But, we felt, it must stop there.

Then, as we read the Scriptures, we found that it did not stop there. In Paul's first letter to the Corinthian church, he wrote: "And in the church God has appointed first of all *apostles*, second prophets, third teachers . . . (1 Cor. 12:28, emphasis mine). And to the church in Rome he wrote: "Greet Andronicus and Junius . . . They are outstanding *among the apostles*, and they were in Christ *before I was*" (Rom. 6:7, emphasis mine).

Apparently, the early Church recognized Christ's calling to apostleship in those individuals. So let's not be quick to say it is wrong to say that God no longer calls apostles today. Only let us be careful to ascertain that they are not "false apostles" such as Paul speaks of in 2 Cor. 11:13-14 and John speaks of in Rev. 2:2.

NOTES

Introduction

1. William M. Ramsay, *The Cities of St. Paul* and *St. Paul the Traveller and the Roman Citizen*. (Grand Rapids, Michigan: Baker Book House, 1960).

Chapter I: Early Life in Tarsus

1. See Appendix I.

Chapter II: Saul Becomes a Pharisee

1. See Appendix IV.

2. See Appendix III.

3. By "Holy Scriptures" Saul meant the Old Testament—the New Testament had not yet been written.

Chapter III: New Markets for Tentmakers

1. Acts 18:2-3 tells of Paulus' first encounter with Aquila and Priscilla. It states that they were tentmakers and that they had recently left Italy because of Emperor Claudius' command for all Christians and Jews to leave Rome. Thus, it is possible that a nephew of Paulus' might have established a business relationship with this couple while they were still in Rome.

Chapter IV: Confrontation in Jerusalem

1. Acts 9:1-6.

2. William M. Ramsay, *The Cities of St. Paul.* (Grand Rapids, Michigan: Baker Book House, 1960), 248.

3. Ibid., 255-259.

4. Acts 14:19-20.

5. William M. Ramsay, *St. Paul the Traveller and the Roman Citizen.* (Grand Rapids, Michigan: Baker Book House, 1960), 197.

6. Ernle Bradford, *Paul the Traveler.* (New York: Macmillan Publishing Co. Inc. 197), 195.

7. See Appendix V.

8. Acts 19:35-41.

9. Acts 16:13-15.

10. Acts 22:7-10.

11. Acts 22:21.

Chapter V: Paulus in Prison in Caesarea

1. Acts 23:12-15.

2. Acts 26:32.

Chapter VI: Shipwreck

1. Acts 27:1-2.

2. Acts 27:6.

3. Acts 27:10-11.

4. Acts 27:12.

5. Acts 27:14 KJV.

6. Acts 27:21-26.

7. Acts 27:39-44.

8. Acts 28:1-8.

9. Acts 28:9-10.

10. Acts 28:10-15.

Chapter VII: Captivity and Trial in Rome

1. Now again we enter a period in the life of Saul of Tarsus (now known as Paulus) when the Bible is silent about his life and work. We only know that he spent at least two years waiting for his trial date, living in his own rented house (under guard), but free to entertain guests and preach to them and writing an occasional letter to one of his churches.

2. Acts 28:17-28.

3. Romans 16:21.

Chapter VIII: Spain and Beyond

1. Ruth 1:16 KJV.

2. Ruth 1:16 KJV.

3. See Appendix VI.

Chapter IX: Final Imprisonment

1. Titus 1:5.

2. Paul had previously sent him an epistle (Titus) giving him valuable information about his duties there and how to conduct the work of the church.

3. See Appendix VII.

4. 2 Timothy 4:6-8.

Chapter X: Jason—the Apostle to Spain

1. Rom. 16:21.

2. 2 Tim. 4:9-10.

3. 2 Tim. 4:9-13.

4. I have seen this story in various forms in my studies of early Spain, but have no written records of it. I believe it is true in the light of repeated accounts, but have no way of verifying the details. The very persistence of the story adds credence to its truth.

5. See Appendix VII.

Appendix I: Was the Apostle Paul Married?

1. Eusebius, *Ecclesiastical History*. (Grand Rapids, Michigan: Baker Book House, 1962), 115.

Appendix V : Diana of the Ephesians

1. Ernle Bradford, *Paul the Traveler*. (New York: Macmillan Publishing Co. Inc., 1974), 194.

2. Ibid., p. 195.

3. Acts 19: 23-41.

Appendix VI: Maimonides

1. "Moses Maimonides Biography." Last updated October 22, 2009. *Who2: http://www.who2.org/mosesmaimonides.html* (October 22, 2009).

2. "Maimonides." Last updated October 16, 2009. *Wikipedia, the Online Encyclopedia: http://en.wikipedia.or/wiki/Maimonides* (October 22, 2009).

3. "Maimonides," *Who2.*

Bibliography

Bradford, Ernle. *Paul the Traveller*. **New York: The Macmillan Publishing Co. Inc., 1974**

Cornfeld, Gaalyahu, ed. *Daniel to Paul.* **New York: The Macmillan Co., 1962.**

Kemp de Money, Netta. *La Geografia Historica del Mundo Biblico.* **Miami: Editorial Vida, 1968.**

Marin, Diego. *La Civilizacion Espanola.* **New York: Holt, Rinehart & Winston. 1969.**

National Geographic Society. *Everyday Life in Bible Times.* **1967.**

Pistonesi, Jose A. *Geografia Biblica de Palestina.* **Buenos Aires: Junta de Publicaciones de la Convencion Bautista.**

Ramsay, Wm. M. *St. Paul the Traveller and the Roman Citizen*. **Grand Rapids: Baker Book House, 1960.**

Ramsay, Wm. M. *The Cities of St. Paul*. **Grand Rapids: Baker Book House, 1960.**

Rivkin, Ellis. *The Shaping of Jewish History: A Radical New Interpretation.* **New York: Charles Scribner's Sons, 1971.**

Tidwell, J. B. *La Geografia Biblica (Version Castellana por Carlos C. Pierson).* **El Paso: Casa Bautista de Publicaciones, 1969.**

Vos, Howard F. *Introduccion a la Arqueologia Biblica.* **Chicago: Editorial Moody.**

Other Books by F. Burleigh Willard Sr.

Streams of Living Water
(with co-author Celia Willard Milslagle)

The Legacy of Frances

Friend of Angels

Overcoming with Christ

LaVergne, TN USA
27 January 2010

171239LV00004B/1/P

9 781449 045272